Border
Town

Border Town

a novel

SHEN CONGWEN

Translated by Jeffrey C. Kinkley

HARPER**PERENNIAL** ● MODERN CHINESE CLASSICS

NEW YORK ● LONDON ● TORONTO ● SYDNEY ● NEW DELHI ● AUCKLAND

HARPER**PERENNIAL** ● MODERNCHINESE**CLASSICS**

HarperCollins books may be purchased for educational, business, or sales
promotional use. For information please write: Special Markets Department,
HarperCollins Publishers, 10 East 53rd Street, New York, NY 10022.

FIRST EDITION

Library of Congress Cataloging-in-Publication Data
    Shen Congwen, 1902–1988.
        [Bian cheng. English]
        Border town : a novel / Shen Congwen ; translated by Jeffrey
C. Kinkley.—1st ed.
            p.   cm.
        ISBN 978-0-06-143691-8
        1. China—Social life and customs—Fiction. I. Title.
    PL2801.N18P513 2009
    895.1'351—dc22   2008056125

09 10 11 12 13   DT/RRD   10 9 8 7 6 5 4 3 2 1

FOREWORD

Once upon a time, Shen Congwen's stories of rural China seemed so close to the lives of the country folk and the grand landscapes framing them that a 1947 collection of his works in English was titled *The Chinese Earth*. That earth was overturned, along with Shen's literary reputation, in the 1949 Communist revolution. Thirty years later, when radical Maoism expired in turn, Chinese critics rediscovered Shen Congwen. They called him the representative writer, perhaps the founder, of a uniquely Chinese prewar school of "native-soil," or "rural," literature. A 1980s revival of Shen's way of combining earthbound themes with ethereal style was accorded partial credit for China's post-Mao literary renaissance.

Those claims created a sensation. Mao's writers had already asserted exclusive understanding of peasants as a class, but the political morality tales they cranked out appear inauthentic today. The themes of nature, agriculture, and cosmic harmony in China's ancient classics and poetry have enjoyed far greater staying power. In the 1920s, however, Shen Congwen and his colleagues declared Classical Chinese and the literature composed in it "dead." They strove to create a New Literature in the modern vernacular, without giving up China's traditional lyric—and didactic—literary missions. Shen Congwen chose the lyric path; *Border Town* (*Bian cheng*), a modern pastoral published in 1934, is his masterpiece. Some call the work implicitly Daoist, but Shen and his generation of writers in principle scorned China's old philosophies. They wanted to be known as moderns, either realist or romantic. Shen Congwen's novels defy classification within that dichotomy, though he, perhaps surprisingly, thought it more a compliment to be called a realist. He liked "revolution" in literary technique, but not as armed struggle for social reconstruction.

These issues explain the fascination with Shen Congwen's views of rural life, even if most critics agree that his greatest contribution to Chinese literature lies in his imagination, craftsmanship, and creation of one of the greatest Chinese prose styles of all time. In the late 1920s and 1930s, China's writers and social scientists "discovered" the Chinese peasant. The loudest literary critics and social ideologues, like their political leaders, were moved by conflict-based theories of class struggle and national survival: Marxism and nationalism, left wing and right wing. Shen Congwen announced at the time that *Border Town* was a tribute to China's farmers and soldiers written in defiance of the ideologues. The Marxists who controlled China's intellectual scene in subsequent decades thought *Border Town* an insult to their ideas of rural class conflict.

It is intriguing to wonder if *Border Town* might also be a Chinese rejoinder to *The Good Earth*. Pearl Buck's novel was controversial in China because it acquired worldwide *authority* to speak for China's peasants, despite its authorship by a foreigner (though Chinese was Buck's first language). An American bestseller of 1931 and 1932, *The Good Earth* won a Pulitzer Prize and was translated into Chinese in 1932. At least two Chinese book versions hit the market in 1933, with more to come before the 1937 release of the celebrated film and Buck's Nobel Prize the next year. The novel's burgeoning success—a *succès de scandale*, some Chinese intellectuals thought—might have hurried up the first English translation of *Border Town* by Emily Hahn and Shao Xunmei in 1936, which inspired Ching Ti and Robert Payne's 1947 version, titled *The Frontier City*, in *The Chinese Earth* anthology. (My translation is indebted to those prior renditions and to a 1981 retranslation by Shen's friend Gladys Yang.)

The Good Earth and *Border Town* depict China's common folk sympathetically. The characters are straightforward, practical, culturally grounded, and hardworking. Moreover, the humble protagonists of both great novels have inner lives, though of the heroines, that is truer of Shen Congwen's Cuicui than of Pearl Buck's stolid O-lan, who suffers far more from gender inequality. The hopes and endeavors of the folk in both novels are "scrutable," even culturally universal, yet subject to being undone by fate.

Since *Border Town*'s resurrection in the 1980s (it was banned in China ca. 1949–1979, and in Taiwan until 1986), many Chinese critics have viewed it as a regional novel. Chadong lies in Shen Congwen's native West Hunan, along not just a provincial boundary but also an internal cultural frontier, where Han Chinese mix with Miao (Hmong), Tujia, and other formerly tribal mountain peoples who once spoke unrelated languages and whose women still wear exotic clothing. According to this reading, the characters in Shen's novel are not ordinary Chinese peasants. Indeed, Shen Congwen preferred to write about small-town boatmen, artisans, soldiers, hunters, and young people, not tillers of the soil. The critics' point, however, is that Shen's characters might belong to the exotic "national minorities" of Southwest China. Some scholars from Chadong's You River Valley argue that Cuicui exemplifies local Tujia culture, whereas critics from the border farther south, where Shen Congwen was born, claim her for the Miao. Her dark skin makes her an exotic beauty within Chinese literature, but darkness is not characteristically "tribal" in that part of China.

Shen Congwen's ancestors were Han, Tujia, and Miao. The fineness of his ethnographic observations and the dialect in some of his other works easily inspire ethnographic interpretations. His youthful clerking for a locally popular West Hunanese warlord and later status as a famous native son have made him a regional hero. One can construct from his works a Chinese Yoknapatawpha—a full and mappable literary landscape like Faulkner's, complete with oppressed minorities acting as conscience to the Han. Yet, markers of ethnic identity are blurred in *Border Town*. That is why scholars can debate Cuicui's ancestry. Minority ethnicity (the Middle Stockade folk would be prime candidates) has been sublimated into a broader, regional, local color. This serves national purposes, for Shen Congwen's West Hunan exemplifies the diversity and creativity of China as a multiethnic universe—a blended nation more than an ethnic mosaic.

Shen Congwen spoke of Freudian influences in *Border Town*, possibly referring to Cuicui's dreams and daydreams, the flute and white pagoda as phalli, or Tianbao and Nuosong as Ego and Id. Although Shen later wrote erotic and experimental stories in a Euro-American high modernist vein, international critics typically see *Border Town* as a conservative work full of idyllic and nostalgic visions and devoted to an exquisite painterly style, an element this translation could not duplicate. Shen Congwen labored tirelessly to rework the modern vernacular into a literary language figuratively as rich as Classical Chinese—when it was "living." The vitality and rawness of youth, balanced by art and nuance, creates tension in much of his writing. In a manifesto of 1936, Shen chided commercialism, faddishness, and politics in contemporary literature, avowing that he only wished "to create a little Greek temple, built of solid stone on a mountain foundation. With economy, vigor, and symmetry as my architectural ideals—in a design perhaps modest, but not fastidious—I would devote this temple to the worship of 'the human spirit.'"

Border Town might be thought a "little Greek temple" in its seeming classicism (neither realist nor romantic), its attention to fate, and its aspect as an eternal modern myth more than a story bounded by time. It is economical in language and plot. Did Shen also achieve his ideal of symmetry? Like many Chinese works of the time, *Border Town* was probably composed a few chapters at a time, just in time for the successive printer's deadlines of its initial serial publication. He began writing in October 1933, deliriously happy at having finally married Zhang Zhaohe, a dark beauty who years earlier had resisted his attentions; she helped inspire the character of Cuicui. The first chapters were published at the start of 1934, but Shen finished writing the novel only after a winter visit to West Hunan, his first in over ten years, to see his dying mother. The land of his childhood now appeared to him spoiled and despoiled. He left in a hurry. Local officials, aware of his criticisms of the Nationalist government, suspected Shen was a Communist. The consistency of *Border Town* is the more remarkable for that.

Shen Congwen was chosen to receive the Nobel Prize for literature in 1988, but he died before the October announcement; the prize necessarily went to another. *Border Town* still occupies a unique place in Chinese and world literature. It inspires one to ponder Shen's favorite subject: the human spirit.

Jeffrey C. Kinkley

Border
Town

CHAPTER ONE

An old imperial highway running east from Sichuan into Hunan province leads, after reaching the West Hunan border, to a little mountain town called Chadong. By a narrow stream on the way to town was a little white pagoda, below which once lived a solitary family: an old man, a girl, and a yellow dog.

As the stream meandered on, it wrapped around a low mountain, joining a wide river at Chadong some three *li* downstream, about a mile. If you crossed the little stream and went up over the heights, you could get to Chadong in one *li* over dry land. The water path was bent like a bow, with the mountain path the bowstring, so the land distance was a little shorter. The stream was about twenty *zhang* wide—two hundred feet—over a streambed of boulders. Though the quietly flowing waters were too deep for a boat pole to touch bottom, they were so clear you could count the fish swimming to and fro. This little stream was a major chokepoint for transit between Sichuan and Hunan, but there was never enough money to build a bridge. Instead the locals set up a square-nosed ferryboat that could carry about twenty passengers and their loads. Any more than that, and the boat went back for another trip. Hitched to a little upright bamboo pole in the prow was a movable iron ring that went around a heavily worn cable spanning the stream all the way to the other side. To ferry across, one slowly tugged on that cable, hand over fist, with the iron ring keeping the boat on track. As the vessel neared the opposite shore, the person in charge would call out, "Steady now, take your time!" while suddenly leaping ashore holding the ring behind. The passengers, with all their goods, their horses, and their cows, would go ashore and head up over the heights, disappearing from view. The ferry landing was owned by the whole community, so the crossing was free to all. Some passengers were a little uneasy about this. When someone grabbed a few coins and threw them down on the boat deck, the ferryman always picked them up, one by one, and pressed them back into the hands of the giver, saying, in a stern, almost quarrelsome voice, "I'm paid for my work: three pecks of rice and seven hundred coppers. That's enough for me. Who needs this charity?"

But that didn't always work. One likes to feel one's done the right thing, and who feels good about letting honest labor go unrewarded? So there were always some who insisted on paying. This, in turn, upset the ferryman, who, to ease his own conscience, sent someone into Chadong with the money to buy tea and tobacco. Tying the best tobacco leaves Chadong had to offer into bundles and hanging them from his money belt, he'd offer them freely and generously to anyone in need. When he surmised from the look of a traveler from afar that he was interested in those tobacco leaves, the ferryman would stuff a few into the man's load, saying, "Elder Brother, won't you try these? Fine goods here, truly excellent; these giant leaves don't look it, but their taste is wonderful— just the thing to give as a gift!" Come June, he'd put his tea leaves into a big earthenware pot to steep in boiling water, for the benefit of any passerby with a thirst to quench.

The ferryman was the old man who lived below the pagoda. Seventy now, he'd kept to his place near this little stream since he was twenty. In the fifty years since, there was simply no telling how many people he'd ferried across in that boat. He was hale and hearty despite his age; it was time for him to have his rest, but Heaven didn't agree. He seemed tied to this work for life. He never mulled over what his work meant to him; he just quietly and faithfully kept on with his life here. It was the girl keeping him company who was Heaven's agent, letting him feel the power of life as the sun rose, and stopping him from thinking of expiring along with the sunlight when it faded at night. His only friends were the ferryboat and the yellow dog; his only family, that little girl.

The girl's mother, the ferryman's only child, had some

fifteen years earlier come to know a soldier from Chadong through the customary exchange of amorous verses, sung by each in turn across the mountain valley. And that had led to trysts carried on behind the honest ferryman's back. When she was with child, the soldier, whose job it was to guard the farmer-soldier colonies upcountry, tried to persuade her to elope and follow him far downstream. But taking flight would mean, for him, going against his military duty, and for her, leaving her father all alone. They thought about it, but the garrison soldier could see she lacked the nerve to travel far away, and he, too, was loath to spoil his military reputation. Though they could not join each other in life, nothing could stop them from coming together in death. He took the poison first. Not steely-hearted enough to ignore the little body growing within her, the girl hesitated. By now her father, the ferryman, knew what was happening, but he said nothing, as if still unaware. He let the days pass as placidly as always. The daughter, feeling shame but also compassion, stayed at her father's side until the child was born, whereupon she went to the stream and drowned herself in the cold waters. As if by a miracle, the orphan lived and matured. In the batting of an eye, she had grown to be thirteen. Because of the compelling deep, emerald green of bamboo stands covering the mountains on either side by the stream where they lived, the old ferryman, without a second thought, named the girl after what was close at hand: Cuicui, or "Jade Green."

Cuicui grew up under the sun and the wind, which turned her skin black as could be. The azure mountains and green brooks that met her eyes turned them clear and bright as crystal. Nature had brought her up and educated her, making her innocent and spirited, in every way like a little wild animal. Yet she was as docile and unspoiled as a mountain fawn, wholly unacquainted with cruelty, never worried, and never angry. When a stranger on the ferry cast a look at her, she would shoot him a glance with those brilliant eyes, as if ready to flee into the hills at any instant; but once she saw that he meant her no harm, she would go back to playing by the waterside as if nothing had happened.

In rainy weather and fair, the old ferryman kept at his post in the prow of the ferryboat. When someone came to cross the stream, he'd stoop to grasp the bamboo cable and use both hands to pull the boat along to the other shore. When he was tired, he stretched out to sleep on the bluffs by the waterside. If someone on the other side waved and hollered that he wanted to cross, Cuicui would jump into the boat to save her grandpa the trouble and swiftly ferry the person across, pulling on the cable smoothly and expertly without a miss. Sometimes, when she was in the boat with her grandpa and the yellow dog, she'd tug the cable along with the ferryman till the boat got to the other side. As it approached the far shore, while the grandfather hailed the passengers with his "Steady now, take your time," the yellow dog would be the first to jump on land, with the tie rope in his mouth. He'd pull the boat to shore with that rope clenched between his teeth, just as if it were his job.

When the weather was clear and fine and there was nothing to do because no one wanted to cross, Grandpa and Cuicui would sun themselves atop the stone precipice in front of their home. Sometimes they'd throw a stick into the water from above and whistle to the yellow dog to jump down from the heights to fetch it. Or Cuicui and the dog would prick up their ears while Grandpa told them stories of war in the city many, many years ago. Other times, they'd each press a little upright bamboo flute to their lips and play the melodies of bridal processions, in which the groom went to the bride's house and brought her home. When someone came to cross, the old ferryman would lay down his flute and ferry the person across on the boat by himself, while the girl, still on the cliff, would call out in a high-pitched voice, just as the boat took off,

"Grandpa, Grandpa, listen to me play. You sing!"

At midstream, Grandpa would suddenly break out in joyful song; his hoarse voice and the reedy sound of the flute pulsated in the still air, making the whole stream seem to stir. Yet the reverberating strains of song brought out the stillness all around.

When the passengers heading for Chadong from East Sichuan included some calves, a flock of sheep, or a bridal

cortege with its ornate palanquin, Cuicui would rush to do
the ferrying. Standing in the boat's prow, she'd move the craft
along the cable languidly and the crossing would be quite
slow. After the calves, sheep, or palanquin were ashore, Cuicui would follow, escorting the pack up the hill, and stand
there on the heights, fixing her eyes on them for a long ways
before she returned to the ferryboat to pull it back to the
shore and home. All alone, she'd softly bleat like the lambs,
low like a cow, or pick wildflowers to bind up her hair like a
bride—all alone.

The mountain town of Chadong was only a *li* from the
ferry dock. When in town to buy oil or salt, or to celebrate
the New Year, the grandfather would stop for a drink. When
he stayed home, the yellow dog would accompany Cuicui as
she went to town for supplies. What she would see in the general store—big piles of thin noodles made from bean starch,
giant vats of sugar, firecrackers, and red candles—made a
deep impression on her. When she got back to her grandfather, she'd go on about them endlessly. The many boats on
the river in town were much bigger than the ferryboat and far
more intriguing, quite unforgettable to Cuicui.

CHAPTER TWO

Chadong was built between the river and the mountains. On the land side, the city wall crept along the mountain contours like a snake. On the water side, tiny boats with awnings berthed along wharves constructed on the land between the wall and the river. Boats heading downstream carried loads of tung oil, rock salt, and nutgalls—the wasp-made swellings on oak trees used to make dyes. Those going upstream transported cotton yarn and cloth, foodstuffs, household supplies, and choice seafood. Threading through each of the wharves was River Street. Land was scarce, so most people's houses were "dangling-foot houses," half on land, half on stilts built over the water. When water crept up over the street during a great springtime flood, the households of River Street would extend long ladders from the eaves of their houses across to the city wall. Cursing and shouting, they'd enter the city over the ladders, carrying cloth-wrapped bundles, bedrolls, and crocks of rice, then wait for the water to recede before coming back out of the city through the gate in the wall. If one year the waters raged especially fierce, the flood might break through the row of stilt houses in one or two places. The onlookers atop the city wall could only gape. Those who suffered the harm stared right back, speechless over their loss, as if it were just one more unhappy and unavoidable act of nature.

When the river flooded, one could watch its sudden swelling from the city wall. Within that vast surge of mountain waters from upstream, houses, oxen, sheep, and giant trees bobbed up and down. In the places where the torrent slowed, as in front of the pontoons by the customs house, people often went out in little sampans. When they spied a head of livestock, a piece of lumber, or a cargoless boat rising and falling in the waves midstream, perhaps with a crying and screaming woman or child on board, they urgently paddled out, and after meeting the object of rescue downstream, lashed it to the sampan with a long rope, then rowed back to shore. These daring souls typified the local people: they had an eye for their own gain, but also for helping other folks. They were equally joyful salvaging people and property, and they did it with such skill and bravery that onlookers felt compelled to shout hurrahs.

The river was the famous You Shui of history, whose new name is the Bai Shui or White River. After the White River got to Chenzhou and merged with the River Yuan, it became somewhat turbid, proving the adage that spring water becomes muddy when it leaves the mountains. Trace the river back upstream, and it was so clear you could see right down to the bottom, through pools thirty or fifty feet deep. When the sun shone on the deep parts, the white pebbles and striated carnelian stones at the bottom were visible clear as could be, along with fish darting to and fro as if floating in air. High mountains came down to the river on both sides—mountains covered with slender bamboos good for making paper, in all seasons such a deep emerald color as to transfix the eyes. Households near the water appeared among peach and apricot blossoms. Come spring, one had only to look: wherever there were peach blossoms there was sure to be a home, and wherever there were people, you could stop for a drink. In the summer, purple cotton-print tunics and trousers that dazzled the eye as they dried in the sunlight became ensigns of human habitation. When autumn and winter arrived, dwellings on the cliffs and by the water came clearly into view—not one could escape notice. Walls of yellow earth and pitch-black tiles, neatly placed there for all time and in harmony with the surroundings on every side, brought the viewer a sense of extraordinary joy. A traveler with the slightest interest in poetry or painting could sail this narrow river curled up in a little boat for a whole month without ever getting tired of it. Miracles could be discovered everywhere. The boldness, the exquisiteness of nature, at every place and every time, led one inescapably into rapture.

The source of the White River was up past the Sichuan frontier. Small boats going upstream could make it all the way on the high waters of spring to Xiushan in Sichuan. Chadong was the last river port on the Hunan side of the border. The big river broadened to half a *li* at Chadong, but when autumn turned to winter and the water level fell, it revealed a riverbed only two hundred feet wide. Beyond that were only shoals of black boulders. Boats arriving at this point could go no farther upstream, so all goods going in or out of East Sichuan had to be unloaded here. Products came out of the province on mulberry wood carrying poles borne on the shoulders of porters. Goods headed the other way had to be tied into bundles for transport by muscle power.

Chadong and its environs were defended by a lone battalion of garrison troops reorganized from the Green Standard Army's farmer-soldiers of yesteryear. They were joined by almost five hundred resident households in town. (Apart from those who owned fields up in the mountains or tung oil presses, and small-time capitalists who gave out loans for tung oil, rice, or cotton yarn, nearly all the others in town were on the military payroll, descended from households brought in to garrison the area.) There was also a *likin* transit-tax bureau, housed in a little temple below River Street outside the city wall. The bureau chief had lived in town for a long time. The battalion of soldiers was quartered in the yamen of the former Green Standard lieutenant-colonel. Were it not for the bugler who blew his daily calls from atop the city wall, reminding all that a garrison was here, one would hardly know that these people were soldiers. On winter days, clothes and green vegetables could be seen drying in the sun in front of every doorway. Sweet potatoes hung from the eaves by their vines. Bags made from palm-bark rain capes, stuffed with chestnuts and hazelnuts, also hung under the eaves. Chickens big and little disported themselves by every house, cackling. Here and there would be a man sitting on the high doorsill of his house or splitting logs with an ax, stacking his firewood in the courtyard in neat piles like pagodas. Middle-aged women wore blue cotton outfits starched stiff, with embroidered white cotton aprons hanging down across their bosoms. They chatted as they worked, stooping in the sunlight. It all reflected eternal peace. Everybody passed each day in a pure quietude that is hard to imagine. This measure of tranquility allowed everyone to consider their personal affairs and also their dreams. Each and every denizen of this small town, within the days allotted by nature, nursed his or her own hopes of love and expectations of hate. But what exactly were they thinking about? That was unfathomable.

Those who lived in the higher elevations within the city walls saw from their front doors scenes of the river and the opposite shore. When a boat approached, they could see innumerable trackers on the opposite bank pulling it upstream. Those trackers brought cakes and imported candies from downriver, which they would exchange for cash in the city after coming ashore. Whenever a boat came to town, the local children's imaginations flew to the men who did the pulling. And the adults? If they'd hatched a nest of chicks or raised a pig or two, they'd entrust them to the towmen on the downstream voyage, to exchange for gold earrings, a few yards of superior black cloth, an earthenware jug of gift-quality soy sauce, or an especially sturdy chimney for their American Standard Oil kerosene lamp. Such thoughts preoccupied most of the housewives.

This small town was peaceful and quiet within its walls, but its location made it the nexus for commerce with East Sichuan, so the little River Street outside the city wall was quite a different story. There were inns where merchants put up and barbers who stayed in place, not just the itinerant ones who set up their chair in the street. There were restaurants, a general store, firms dealing in tung oil and salt, and a shop selling cloth of all designs and colors—every kind of merchandise had found its place along this River Street. Still another outfit sold hardwood pulleys, bamboo cables, woks and pots, all for use onboard ships. And wharf rats made their living connecting the boatmen with their employers. Long tables in front of the little restaurants offered carp fried a crispy brown, lying in a big shallow earthenware bowl with bean curd, the fish adorned with slivers of red peppers. Next to the bowl was a big bamboo cylinder with giant red chopsticks sticking up out of it. Anyone willing to plunk down the money could edge up to that table outside the front door, take a seat, and pull out a pair of those chopsticks. A woman with a white powdered face and finely plucked eyebrows would come over and ask, "Elder Brother, Honorable Soldier, what'll it be? Sweet wine? Clear liquor?" A male customer who was witty and wanted to get a rise out of her, or who fancied the proprietress a little, would feign anger and retort, "Sweet wine, for the likes of me? Do I look like a child? Sweet wine, you say!" Potent white spirits were then dipped out of the wine vat with a wooden ladle into an earthenware bowl set immediately upon the table. This bowl of spirits was of course strong and pungent, enough to knock out many a stout fellow, so one couldn't drink another.

The general store sold American kerosene, the Standard Oil lamps that burned it, incense, candles, and paper goods. The oil firm was a depot for tung oil. The salt firm stored piles of rock salt of the sort produced since ancient times in Huojing town, Sichuan. The dry goods shop sold white cotton yarn, cloth, cotton, and the black silk crepe wound around the head as a turban. The ship chandler had just about everything in its trade, sometimes even an anchor weighing a hundred catties just resting outside the door and waiting for a customer to ask its price. Boat owners clad in their dark blue sateen mandarin jackets and fidgeting boatmen went in and out of the establishment of the wharf rats who got the boatmen their work; its door, on River Street, was open all day long. It was like a teahouse that sold no tea, though you could smoke a pipe of opium there. The men all said they went there to keep up on their trade, but everybody in the crew from top to bottom, from the oarsmen on board to the trackers onshore, observed a rule: no talking about numbers. Most went there to "socialize." With the "Dragon Head" lodge master at the center of things, they talked about local affairs, business conditions in the two provinces, and "news," most of which came from downriver. Meetings and fund-raising generally took place here, and it was here, too, that money-savers' circles often threw the dice to see who took home the pot this time. The trades that really held their attention were two in number: the buying and selling of boats, and of women.

Certain kinds of big-city hangers-on follow commercial prosperity, to meet the needs of merchants and also the boatmen. Even this tiny border town had those types along its River Street; they congregated in establishments housed in the dangling-foot structures. These little dames were either brought in from the surrounding countryside or they were camp followers of the Sichuan Army when it had come foraging in Hunan. They wore jackets of faux foreign satin over cotton print trousers; they plucked their eyebrows into thin lines and drew up their hair into big topknots that gave off strong scents of cheaply perfumed oil. Unoccupied during the day, they sat outside their doorways on little square stools, making shoes to while away the time, embroidering mating phoenixes on the toes in red and green silk thread and keeping an eye out for passersby. Or they'd sit by a window along the river to watch the sailors lifting cargo and listen to them sing as they climbed up the masts. Come evening, though, they'd take their turns serving the merchants and the boatmen, earnestly doing all that it was a prostitute's duty to do.

Folkways in a border district are so straightforward and unsophisticated that even the prostitutes retained their everlasting honesty and simplicity. With a new customer, they got the money in advance; with business settled, they closed the door and the wild oats were sown. If they knew the customer, payment was up to him. The prostitutes depended on the Sichuan merchants for their living, but their love went to the boatmen. When the couple were sweet on each other, they'd each swear an oath when parting, biting each other on the lips and the nape of the neck, promising to stay true during their separation. The one afloat on the boat, and likewise the one staying ashore, got through the next forty, the next fifty days with their heartstrings firmly bound to the other so far away. Particularly the women, who were given to true infatuations of indescribable simplemindedness, would see their man in their dreams if he failed to return within the agreed-upon time. Often they'd envision the boat pull into shore and their man teeter on his sea legs down the gangplank, then come running directly to her side. If she'd begun to doubt him, she'd see the man up in the rigging, directing his songs toward another quarter and ignoring her. The weaker spirits would proceed to dream of drowning themselves in the river or taking an overdose of opium, whereas those made of sterner stuff would run at their man with a cleaver. Though far outside the bounds of ordinary society, when tears and laughter worked their way into these women's lives through loves won and loves lost, they were just like women of any other time or place, ruled body and soul by love and hate, with all their chills and fevers, oblivious to all else. The only thing really setting them apart was that they were a little more given to resolve, and therefore also foolishness—just that, no more. Short-term commitments, long-term engagements, one-night stands—these transactions with women's bodies, given the simplicity of local mores, did not feel degrading or shameful to those who did business with their bodies, nor did those on the outside use the concepts of the educated to censure them or look down on them. These women put principles before profit and they kept their promises; even if they *were* prostitutes, they tended to be more trustworthy than city people who knew all about "shame."

The man in charge of the docks was one Shunshun, a character who'd spent his time in the ranks during the Qing dynasty and then led a squad as a sergeant in the famous Forty-ninth army regiment at the time of the revolution. Others of his rank had either become famous for their revolutionary exploits or lost their heads, but he went home, though with bad feet—the result of gout from youthful carousing. He bought a simple six-man wooden boat with his modest savings and rented it out to a boat captain down on his luck to transport goods between Chadong and Chenzhou on commission. Luck was with him; the boat sailed safely, and in six months he'd saved money enough to marry a pretty, black-haired young widow. That was his start. Several years later, he had acquired eight boats that plied the river, a wife, and two sons.

This untrammeled and free-spending fellow, able though he was in business, liked to store up friends and give out money. Shunshun was always there for those in need, so he never became greatly rich like the tung oil merchants. He knew what it was like to live on army rations and endure the hardships of travel, and what it felt like to have one's hopes dashed. Whenever a boat owner bankrupted by a shipwreck, a demobilized soldier on his way home, or a scholar or painter wanting to study abroad came to town for help because he'd heard of Shunshun's generosity, he did his utmost for them, one and all. He earned his fortune from the water, and so he sprinkled that fortune all around. He could swim, even with his bad feet. His walk was uneven, but his character and judgments were straightforward, right down the middle. Things were fairly simple out on the river; everything was decided by customary practice. Which boat was at fault in a collision, which boat had harmed another's property—usually there was an established way to decide it. But to apply all these customary laws they needed an elder of tested virtue. On an autumn day some years before, the old boss of the riverfront had passed away. Shunshun took his place. He was only fifty at the time, but he was so astute, upright, and even-tempered, so free of greed and venality, that no objections were heard on account of his youth.

His older son was now already seventeen years old; the younger, fifteen. These young men were as strong and muscular as little bulls. They could pilot boats and they could swim and hike long distances. Anything a lad who had grown up in a country town could do, they could do, and expertly. The older was more like his father in temper—bold, unconstrained, and confident, not tied down by pettiness or convention. The younger one's personality followed that of his pretty and delicate mother. He was not so given to talk, and his eyebrows were exquisite and forceful—one look at him and you knew he was intelligent and full of passion.

Now that the brothers had grown up, it was time to test their characters in every different line of work. The father had sent each boy in turn on journeys to distant parts. When taking a boat downstream, they suffered the same hardships as the rest of the crew. When it was time to man the oars, they chose the heaviest one, and when it was time for towing, they took the lead place among the trackers. They ate the same dried fish, hot peppers, and putrid pickled cabbage as the others, and they slept on the same stiff, hard deck planks. On the land route upriver, taking the East Sichuan trade route, they did business in Xiushan, Longtan, and Youyang, always on schedule, even while wearing straw sandals in heat and cold, rain and snow. The young men were armed with knives. They could unsheathe them in a flash, but did so only when forced. They'd move to a clearing and wait for the opponent to make his move, then let their muscles decide the outcome. Gang ritual decreed that "it takes a knife both to fend off adversaries and make blood brothers," so when a knife was needed, the two boys were not shy about putting it to its intended use. All their education—in the ways of trade, social manners, living in a strange environment, using a knife to defend their persons and their reputations—seemed aimed at teaching these two boys the courage and sense of duty to be a man. And this very education made both of them as strong and tough as tigers, yet also friendly and approachable, never lazy and arrogant, ostentatious, or bullying. When anyone at the Chadong frontier brought up the character of Shunshun and his boys, they always spoke their names with respect.

Since his boys' infancy, their father had seen that the elder would resemble him in all things, yet he seemed slightly partial to the younger son. This unconscious preference led him to name the elder son Tianbao (Heaven-protected), and his younger brother Nuosong (Sent by the Nuo Gods). He who was protected by Heaven might not be so favored in the worldly affairs of humans, but he who was sent by the Nuo gods, according to local understanding, must not be underestimated. Nuosong was exquisitely handsome. The boat people of Chadong were hard put to find words for his good looks. The best they could come up with was the nickname Yue Yun. None of them had ever seen Yue Yun, that most handsome warrior of the Song dynasty a thousand years earlier, but they thought they saw a resemblance to the dashing Yue Yun figure who appeared onstage in local opera.

CHAPTER THREE

For ten years and more, the local military commander at this provincial border had emphasized maintaining the peace and keeping things as they were. He handled things quite deftly, so there had been no unrest. Commerce on land and water never had to stop on account of warfare or rural banditry; good order was the rule, and people were satisfied. They felt grief at such misfortunes as the death of a cow, the capsizing of a boat, or any other fatal catastrophe, but the disasters suffered by other places in China due to the awful struggles going on there seemed never to be felt by these frontier folk.

The most stirring days of the year in this border town were the Dragon Boat Festival, the Mid-autumn Festival, and the lunar New Year. These three festival days excited the people here exactly as they had fifty years before. They were still the days that meant the most.

At the Dragon Boat Festival on the fifth day of the fifth lunar month, women and children put on new clothes and

painted the character *wang*, or "king," on their foreheads
using wine mixed with realgar. Everybody got to eat fish and
meat this day. By eleven o'clock in the morning, all Chadong
was sitting down to lunch, after which those who lived in
town locked their doors and went down to the riverside to see
the dragon boats race. If they knew people on River Street,
they could watch from the houses on stilts overhanging the
river. Otherwise, they watched from in front of the customs
house or from one of the many piers. The dragon boat race
began downstream at the Long Depths stretch of the river.
The finish line was in front of the customs house. The local
military officers, customs officials, and all people of impor-
tance gathered at the customs house this day to take in the
excitement. The oarsmen had prepared for the race days in
advance, with each competing team selecting its strongest
and nimblest young lads to practice their maneuvers in the
deep part of the river. The dragon boats were longer and nar-
rower than ordinary wooden boats, with upturned ends and
a long vermilion stripe painted on the hull. Most of the year
they were stored in dry caves by the river. When it came time
to use them, they were towed out into the water. Each boat sat
twelve to eighteen oarsmen, a helmsman, and two men to beat
the drum and gong. The oarsmen's short paddles rowed the
boat forward to the rhythm of the drumbeats—first unhur-
ried, then urgent. The red-turbaned cox sat in the prow waving two little signal flags left and right, directing the motion

of the boat. The men who pounded the drum and beat the gong usually sat amidships. The moment the boat launched, they started up the single-minded booming and clanging that governed the speed with which the boatmen thrust their oars into the river. The boat's speed had to follow the sound of the drum and gong, so whenever two boats got to the climax of their competition, the thunder of the percussion, added to the encouraging cheers from both banks, recalled novels and stories about Liang Hongyu beating her drum in the historic naval battle at Laoguan River, and the cacophony when Niu Gao fished the rebel Yang Yao out of the water. All who rowed their boat to victory were rewarded at the finish line in front of the customs house with red silk and a little silver badge, not just for their individual efforts but to acknowledge the boat's glorious teamwork. Soldiers used to taking things into their own hands felt compelled to congratulate the victorious boat by setting off strings of five-hundred-pop firecrackers.

After the race, the garrison soldiers and officers in town, to make common cause with the citizenry and increase the merriment of all concerned, released green-headed drakes out on the river with red ribbons tied around their long necks, so that the best swimmers, be they soldiers or civilians, could jump into the river and catch them. Anyone who captured a duck got to keep it. Thereupon the river at Long Depths hosted a unique spectacle: a stream simply covered with ducks—and people swimming after them.

These competitions, of boat against boat and man against duck, went on until the day was done.

Dragon Head Elder Brother Shunshun, now boss of the riverfront, had been an expert swimmer in his youth. When he dove into the water to catch a drake, he never went home empty-handed. But it came to be that during one festival, when his younger son, Nuosong, had turned eleven and was able to hold his breath long enough to swim to a drake under water and catch him by surprise, the father said to his son, a little defensively, "All right, it's up to you two now, no need for me to dive in anymore!" And that was the end of his jumping into the water to compete in catching ducks. Diving in to save a life, of course, was a different matter. He would jump into fire itself to save a person from calamity. You could be sure he would consider it his bounden duty even when he was eighty!

Now Tianbao and Nuosong were the best rowers around, the top picks.

The Dragon Boat Festival on the fifth of the month was about to come around, so a big meeting was held on River Street on the first. The neighborhood decided then to launch the boat that belonged to their street. It happened that Tianbao was on an upcountry journey that day, accompanying merchants on the land route to East Sichuan to sell festival goods in Longtan. Only Nuosong could attend the meeting. Sixteen strapping young men, strong as oxen, journeyed upriver to the mountain cave where the boats were hidden, carrying incense, candles, firecrackers, and a drum on legs, whose rawhide drumheads had the circular yin-yang symbol painted in vermilion. Ceremoniously, they lit incense and candles and pulled their boat into the river. Then they boarded it, exploding firecrackers and beating the drum. The boat swept downstream, swift as an arrow, to the Long Depths.

That was in the morning. After noon, the dragon boat of the fisher folk on the other shore was launched, too; the two boats began to practice all sorts of competitive maneuvers. The very first drumbeats coming from the river brought joy to those who heard them, a sign that the festival was close at hand. Denizens of the houses on stilts near the river began to think of their man's return, or began to hope for it, or at the very least were stimulated by the drumming to remember him. Many boats would be home for the festival, but others would have to pass the day away from home. This was a time when you could see feelings of delight and sorrow you ordinarily didn't get to see. Along the River Street of this little mountain town, some people were beaming; others were frowning.

When the booming of the drums skimmed over the water and crossed the hills to the ferryboat, the first to hear it was the yellow dog. Startled, he ran wildly around the house in circles, yapping all the way. When someone ferried across the stream to the eastern bank, he followed and ran up the hill with them, barking toward the town.

Cuicui was sitting on the great rocky bluffs outside her door, weaving grasshoppers and centipedes from palm leaves to amuse herself, when she saw the yellow dog suddenly awaken from his sleep under the sun and run around as if possessed, then cross the stream and come back. She scolded him,

"Hey there, dog! What's gotten into you? Stop it!"

But soon she made out the sound herself. She, too, ran around the house, then ferried herself and the dog across the stream, where she stood with him on the hilltop and listened for the longest time, letting those entrancing drumbeats carry her away to a festival in the past.

CHAPTER FOUR

I t was two years earlier: at festival time, on the fifth day of the fifth month, Grandpa found someone to replace him at the ferry and took the yellow dog and Cuicui into town to see the boat race. The riverbanks were crowded with people as four long, red boats slipped across the river depths. The "Dragon Boat tide" that raised the waters, the pea-green color of the stream, the bright, clear day, and the booming of the drums had Cuicui pursing her lips in silence, though her heart swelled with inexpressible joy. It was so crowded, with everyone straining to see what was happening on the river, that before long, though the yellow dog remained at Cuicui's side, Grandpa was jostled away out of sight.

Cuicui kept watching the boat race, thinking to herself that her grandfather was bound to come back soon. But a long time passed and he failed to return. Cuicui began to feel a little panicky. When the two of them had come to town the day before with the yellow dog, Grandpa had asked Cuicui,

"Tomorrow is the boat race: if you go into town by yourself to see it, will you be afraid of the crowd?" Cuicui replied, "Crowds don't scare me, but it's no fun to watch the race by yourself." At that, her grandfather thought it over and finally remembered an old friend in town. He went that night to ask the old man to come tend the ferryboat for the day so he could bring Cuicui to town. Since the other man was even more alone than the old ferryman, without a relative to his name— not even a dog—it was agreed that he'd come over in the morning for a meal and a cup of realgar wine. The next day arrived; with the meal finished and the ferry duty handed over to the other man, Cuicui and her family entered the town. It occurred to Grandpa to ask along the way, once again: "Cuicui, with so many people down there, and so much commotion, do you dare go down to the riverbank to watch the dragon boats alone?" Cuicui answered, "Of course I do! But what's the point of watching it alone?" Once they got to the river, the four vermilion boats at Long Depths mesmerized Cuicui. She forgot all about her grandfather. He thought to himself, "This will take some time; it'll be another three hours before it's over. My friend back at the ferry deserves to see the young people whoop it up. I ought to go back and trade places with him. There's plenty of time." So he told Cuicui, "It's crowded, so you stay right in this spot. I have to go do something, but I'll be sure to get back in time to take you home." Cuicui was spellbound by the sight of two boats racing prow-to-prow, so she agreed without taking in what her grandpa had said. Realizing that the yellow dog at Cuicui's side might well be more reliable than he, the old man returned home to the ferry.

When he arrived, Grandpa saw his old friend standing below the white pagoda, listening to the distant sound of the drums.

Grandpa hailed him to bring the boat over so the two could ferry across the brook and stand under the pagoda together. The friend asked why the old ferryman had returned in such a hurry. Grandpa told him he wanted to spell him a while. He'd left Cuicui by the shore so his friend could also enjoy the excitement down at the big river. He added, "If you like the spectacle, no need to return, just tell Cuicui to come home when it's over. If my little girl is afraid to come by herself, you can accompany her back!" Grandpa's stand-in had long ago lost any interest in watching dragon boats; he'd rather stay here with the ferryman on the big bluffs by the stream and drink a cup or two of wine. The old ferryman was quite happy to hear that. He took out his gourd of wine and gave it to his friend from town. They reminisced about Dragon Boat Festivals past as they drank. Pretty soon the friend drank himself to sleep, out on the rock.

Having succumbed to the liquor, he could hardly return to town. Grandpa couldn't very well abandon his post at the ferry, either. Cuicui, who was stranded at the river, began to worry.

The boat race achieved its final outcome and the military

officers in town sent a boat into the Long Depths to release the ducks. Still Grandpa was nowhere to be seen. Fearing that her grandfather might be waiting for her somewhere else, Cuicui and the yellow dog made their way through the crowd, and still there was no trace of him. Soon it would be twilight. All the soldiers from town who'd come hefting benches to watch the commotion had shouldered them now and returned home, one by one. Only three or four ducks remained at liberty in the river. The number of people chasing them was dwindling, too. The sun was setting, in the direction of Cuicui's home upstream. Dusk draped the river in a thin coat of mist. A terrible thought suddenly occurred to Cuicui as she surveyed this scene: "Could Grandpa be dead?"

Keeping in mind that Grandpa had asked her to stay in this spot, she tried to disprove the awful thought to herself by imagining that he must have gone into town and run into an acquaintance, maybe been dragged off to have a drink. That was why he hadn't come back. Because it really was a possibility, she didn't want to leave for home with the yellow dog when it wasn't completely dark yet. She could only keep on waiting for her grandpa there by the stone pier.

Soon two long boats from the other shore moved into a small tributary and disappeared. Nearly all the spectators had dispersed, too. The prostitutes in the houses on stilts lit their lanterns and some of them were already singing to the sound of tambourines and lutes. From other establishments came the raucous shouting of men drinking during the guess-fingers game. Meanwhile, in boats moored below the stilt houses, people were frying up dishes for a feast; greens and turnips sizzled in oil as they plopped into their woks. The river was already obscured by the misty darkness. Only a solitary white duck was still afloat on the river, with just one person chasing it.

Cuicui stayed by the dockside, still believing that her grandfather would come to take her home.

As the strains of song coming from the stilt houses grew louder, she heard talking on a boat below, and a boatman saying, "Jinting, listen, that's *your* whore, singing to some merchant from Sichuan while he downs his liquor! I'll bet a finger on it, that's her voice!" Another boatman replied, "Even when she sings drinking songs for other men, she's still thinking of me! She knows I'm in this boat!" The first added, "So she gives her body to other people, but her heart stays with you? How do you know?" The other said, "I'll prove it to you!" Whereupon he gave a strange whistle. The singing above stopped, and the boatmen had a good laugh. They had a good deal to say about the woman after that, much of it obscene. Cuicui was not used to such language, but she couldn't leave the spot. Not only that, she heard one of the boatmen say that the woman's father had been stabbed at Cotton Ball Slope— seventeen times. That uncomfortable thought suddenly seized her again: "Could Grandpa be dead?"

As the boatmen continued conversing, the remaining white drake in the pool swam slowly toward the pier where Cuicui stood. She thought to herself, "Come any closer and I'll catch you!" She kept waiting there quietly, but when the duck came within ten yards of the shore, someone laughed and hailed the sailors on the boat. A third person was still in the water. He grabbed the duck and was slowly making his way to shore, treading water. Hearing the shouting from the river, a man on the boat yelled back into the murky haze, "Hey, No. 2, you're really something! That's the fifth one you've bagged today." The one in the water replied, "This character was really clever, but I caught him anyway." "It's ducks for you today, and tomorrow women—I'll bet you'll be just as good at that." The one in the water fell silent and swam up to the pier. As he climbed up onshore, dripping wet, the yellow dog at Cuicui's side yapped at him as a warning. It was then that he noticed Cuicui. She was the only one on the dock now.

"Who are you?" he asked.

"Cuicui."

"And who might that be?"

"The granddaughter of the ferryman at Bixiju, Green Creek Hill."

"What are you doing here?"

"Waiting for my grandpa. He's coming to get me."

"It doesn't look like he's coming. Your grandfather must

have gone into town for a drink at the army barracks. I'll bet he passed out and someone carried him home!"

"He wouldn't do any such thing. He said he'd come get me, so that's what he'll do."

"This is no place to wait for him. Come up to my house, over there where the lamps are lit. You can wait for him there. How about that?"

Cuicui mistook his good intentions in inviting her to his home. Recalling the revolting things the sailors had said about that woman, she thought the boy wanted her to go up into one of those houses with the singing girls. She'd never cursed before, but she was on edge, having waited so long for her grandfather. When she heard herself invited to go upstairs to his home, she felt insulted and said, softly,

"Damned low-life! You're headed for the executioner!"

She said it under her breath, but the boy heard it, and he could tell from her voice how young she was. He smiled at her and said, "What, are you cursing me? If you want to wait here instead of coming with me, and a big fish comes up and bites you, don't expect me to rescue you!"

Cuicui answered, "If a fish does bite me, that's nothing to you."

As if aware that Cuicui had been insulted, the yellow dog began barking again. The boy lunged at the dog with the duck to scare him, then walked off toward River Street. The dog wanted to chase him, having now been insulted himself, when Cuicui yelled, "Hey, boy, save your barks for when they're needed!" Her meaning seemed to be, "That joker isn't worth barking at," but the young man thought he heard something else, to the effect that the dog should not bark at a well-meaning person. He was wreathed in smiles as he disappeared from view.

A while later, someone came over from River Street to fetch Cuicui, bearing a torch made from leftover rope and calling her name. But when she saw his face, Cuicui didn't recognize him. He explained that the old ferryman had gone home and could not come to retrieve her, so he'd sent a message back with a passenger for Cuicui to return home at once. When Cuicui heard that her grandfather had sent the man, she went home with him, skirting the city wall and letting him lead the way with his torch. The yellow dog sometimes went in front, sometimes in back. Along the way, Cuicui asked the man how he'd known she was still there by the river. He said No. 2 had told him; he worked in No. 2's household. When he got her home, he'd have to return to River Street.

Cuicui asked, "How did No. 2 know I was there?"

Her guide smiled and said, "He was out on the river catching ducks and he saw you by the dock on his way home. He asked you, innocently enough, to go home and sit a while in his house until your grandpa came, but you swore at him! And your dog barked at him, having no idea who he was!"

Surprised at this, Cuicui asked, softly, "Who is No. 2?"

Now it was the worker's turn to be surprised: "You've never heard of No. 2? He's Nuosong! We call him No. 2 on River Street. He's our Yue Yun! And he asked me to take you home!"

Nuosong was not an unfamiliar name in Chadong!

When Cuicui thought of her curse words a while ago, she felt stunned and also ashamed. There was nothing she could say. She followed the torchbearer silently.

When they'd rounded the hill and could see the lamplight in the house across the stream, the ferryman spotted the torchlight where Cuicui was. He immediately set out with his boat, calling out in his hoarse voice, "Cuicui, Cuicui, is it you?" Cuicui didn't answer her grandpa, but only said, under her breath, "No, it's not Cuicui, not her, Cuicui was eaten by a big fish in the river long ago." When she was in the boat, the man sent by No. 2 left with his torch. Grandpa pulled on the ferry cable and asked, "Cuicui, why didn't you answer me? Are you angry at me?"

Cuicui stood in the prow and still said not a word. Her irritation at her granddad dissipated when she got home across the creek and saw how drunk the other old man was. But something else, which had to do with her and not her grandfather, kept Cuicui in silence through the rest of the night.

CHAPTER FIVE

Two years passed.

It happened that during neither of those years' Mid-autumn Festivals, when the moon should have been at its fullest, was there any moon to be seen. None of the exploits of young girls and boys singing love songs to each other all night under the moonlight, customary in this border town, could take place. Hence the two Mid-autumn Festivals had made only a very faint impression on Cuicui. But during the last two New Year's celebrations, she could see soldiers and villagers put on lion dances and processions of dragon lanterns on the parade grounds to welcome in the spring. The sound of the drums and gongs was exciting and raucous. At the end of the festival on the evening of the fifteenth of the first month, the garrison soldiers who had frolicked inside the lions and dragons traveled all over, bare-chested, braving the fireworks. At the army encampment in town, at the residence of the head customs inspector, and in some of the bigger establishments on River Street, everyone cut thin bamboos or hollowed out palm tree roots and stems, then mixed saltpeter with sulfur, charcoal, and steel powder to make thousand-pop firecrackers. Daring and fun-loving soldiers, stripped to the waist, came waving their lanterns and beating their drums as packs of little firecrackers dangling from poles sent sparks down their backs and shoulders like rain showers. The quickening beat of drums and gongs sent the crowd into a frenzy. When the bursts of firecrackers were over, the crowd fired rockets from great tubes anchored to the feet of long benches, setting them off with fuses that extended into an open field. First came a white light with a sizzle. Slowly, slowly, the sizzle changed into a great howl, like a frightening clap of thunder and the roar of a tiger, as the white light shot up two hundred feet into the air. Then it showered the whole sky with multicolored sparks thick as droplets of rain. The soldiers brandishing lanterns went around in circles, oblivious to the sparks. Cuicui witnessed this excitement with her grandfather and it made an impression on her, but inexplicably, it was not as sweet and beautiful as that left by the day of the dragon boats two years before.

Unable to forget that day, Cuicui had gone back to River Street with her grandpa the year before and watched the boats for some time. Just when everything was going fine, it suddenly began to rain, soaking everyone to the bone. To escape the rain, grandfather and granddaughter, with the yellow dog, had gone up into Shunshun's stilt house, where they crowded into a corner. Someone passed by them carrying a stool; Cuicui recognized him as the man with the torch who had led her home. She said to her grandfather:

"Grandfather, that's the man who brought me home last year. Walking along the path with a torch like that, he was just like a highwayman!"

At first Grandpa said nothing, but when the man turned his head and approached, the ferryman grabbed him and said, grinning widely,

"Hey, there, you old highwayman, I asked you to stay for a drink but you wouldn't stay put! Were you afraid of poison? Did you think I dared to slay a true-born Son of Heaven?"

When the man saw that it was the ferryman, and then caught sight of Cuicui, he grinned. "Cuicui, how you've grown! No. 2 said a big fish might eat you if you stayed by the riverbank, but our river doesn't have any fish big enough to swallow you now!"

Cuicui said not a word. She puckered her lips and smiled. She heard this old highwayman speak No. 2's name, but the boy was nowhere to be seen. From the conversation between her grandfather and the other elder, Cuicui gathered that No. 2 was spending the Dragon Boat Festival two hundred miles downstream, at the Qinglang or Green Foam Rapids of the River Yuan. But this festival she got to see No. 1 and also the famous Shunshun. The old ferryman praised a fat duck that No. 1 brought home after catching it on the river, praised it twice, so Shunshun told him to give it to Cuicui. And when he learned how hard up their household was—too poor to wrap their own *zongzi* dumplings for the festival—he gave them a big lot of the three-cornered treats.

While that notable of the waterways conversed with her grandfather, Cuicui pretended to be looking at the events in the river, but really she was taking in every word. The other man said that Cuicui had grown quite beautiful. He asked her age, and whether she was promised to anyone. Her grandfather gleefully bragged about her, but seemed reluctant to broach the topic of her marriage prospects. He didn't breathe a word about that.

On the way home, Grandpa carried the white duck and other goods, while Cuicui led the way with a torch. The two made their way along the foot of the city wall, between the wall and the river. Grandpa said: "Shunshun is a good man, extremely generous. No. 1 is like him. The whole family is quite fine!" Cuicui asked, "Do you know everyone in the family?" Grandpa didn't see what she was driving at. The day had raised his spirits so much that he went ahead and asked, smiling, "Cuicui, if No. 1 wanted to take you as his wife and sent over a matchmaker, would you agree?" Cuicui replied, "Grandfather, you're crazy! Keep on like this and I'll get angry!"

Grandpa said no more, but clearly he was still mulling

over this silly and inopportune idea. Cuicui, aggravated, ran up ahead, swinging the torch wildly from side to side.

"Don't be angry, Cuicui, I might fall into the river. This duck might get away!"

"Who wants that old duck?"

Realizing why she was angry, Grandpa began singing a shanty the oarsmen used to speed their rowing while they shot the rapids. His voice was rasping, but the words were clear as could be. Cuicui kept going as she listened, then suddenly stopped and asked:

"Grandfather, is that boat of yours going down the Green Foam Rapids?"

Grandpa didn't answer, he just kept on singing. Both of them recalled that Shunshun's No. 2 was spending the holiday on a boat at the Green Foam Rapids, but neither knew what the other was implying. Grandfather and granddaughter walked home in silence. As they neared the ferry, the man tending the boat for them brought it to the bank to await their arrival. They crossed the stream to go home, then ate the *zongzi*. When it came time for the man to go back to town, Cuicui was quick to light a torch for him so he could see his way home. As he crossed over the hill, Cuicui and her grandfather watched him from the boat. She said,

"Grandfather, look, the highwayman has gone back into the hills!"

As he pulled the boat along the cable, his eyes trained on

the mist that had suddenly come up from the stream, Grandpa acted as if he'd seen something and softly sighed. He quietly tugged the boat toward home on the opposite bank and let Cuicui go ashore first, while he stayed by the boat. It was a festival day. He knew that country folk would still be returning home in the dark after seeing the dragon boats in town.

CHAPTER SIX

One day the old ferryman got into an argument with a passenger, a seller of wrapping paper. The one refused to accept money proffered and the other insisted on paying. The old ferryman felt a little bullied by the merchant's attitude, so he put on a show of anger and forced the man to take back his money—pressed the coins right back into his hand. But when the boat reached the shore, the traveler jumped up onto the dock and cast a handful of coppers back into the boat, smiling gleefully before hurrying off on his way. The old ferryman had to keep steadying the boat till the other passengers made it ashore, so he couldn't pursue the merchant. Instead, he called out to his granddaughter, who was up on the hill:

"Cuicui, grab hold of that cheeky young paper-seller and don't let him go!"

Cuicui had no idea what was going on, but she went with the yellow dog to block the way of the first passenger off the boat. He laughed and said,

"Let me pass!"

As he spoke, a second merchant caught up with them and told Cuicui what it was all about. She understood and held on to the paper merchant's gown for dear life, insisting, "You can't go, you can't!" To show his agreement with his mistress, the yellow dog, too, began barking at the man. The other traveling merchants were blocked for a while, but they all had a good laugh. Grandpa came up in an angry huff, forced the money back into the man's hand, and even stuck a big wad of tobacco leaves into the merchant's load. He rubbed his hands together and beamed: "Go on, now! Hit the road, all of you!" And at that, they all went on their way, chuckling.

"Grandfather, I thought you were quarreling with that man because he'd stolen from you!" Cuicui said.

Her grandfather replied,

"He gave me money, a lot of it. I don't want his money! I told him that and still he bickered with me about it. He just wouldn't listen to reason!"

"Did you give it all back to him?" Cuicui asked.

Grandpa shook his head and pouted. Then he winked and smiled knowingly, taking out from his belt the lone copper he had stuffed there. He gave it to Cuicui and said,

"He got some tobacco from me in return. He can smoke that all the way to Zhen'gan town!"

The pounding of faraway drums could be heard, and the yellow dog pricked up his ears. Cuicui asked Grandpa if he could hear it. He strained his ears and recognized the sound.

"Cuicui, the Dragon Boat Festival has come around again. Do you remember how last year Master Tianbao gave you a fat duck to take home? This morning First Master went off on business with his crew to East Sichuan. On the ferry he asked about you. I'll bet you forgot all about the downpour last year. If we go this time, we'll have to light a torch again to come home. Do you remember how the two of us came home, lighting our way with a torch?"

Cuicui was just then thinking about the other Dragon Boat Festival, two years ago. But when her grandfather asked, she shook her head, slightly annoyed, and said, pointedly: "I don't remember it, not at all. I can't remember anything about it!" What she really meant was, "How could I have forgotten?"

Knowing full well what she really meant, Grandpa added, "The festival two years ago was even more interesting. You waited for me alone by the riverbank. It got dark and you were just about lost. I thought a big fish must have eaten you all up!"

Recalling this, Cuicui snickered.

"Grandfather, are you the one who thought a big fish might eat me? It was someone else who said that about me, and I told you! All you cared about that day was getting that old man from town to drink all the wine in your gourd! Some memory you have!"

"I'm old and my memory is completely gone. Cuicui, you've

grown up now. You'll have no trouble going into town alone to see the boats race. No need to worry about a fish eating you."

"Now that I'm older, I ought to stay and mind the ferry-boat."

"It's when you get really old that you stay with the ferry-boat."

"When you get old, you deserve a rest!"

"Your grandfather isn't so old! I can still hunt tigers!" Grandpa said, flexing his biceps and making a muscle to show how young and strong he still was. "Cuicui, if you don't believe me, see if you can bite through this!"

Cuicui cast a sidelong glance at her grandpa, whose back was slightly hunched. She didn't reply. Far away, she heard the sound of *suona* horns. She knew what that meant. She could tell the direction it was coming from. She asked her grandpa to get in the boat with her and go to the other side, where their house was. To get a look at the bride's palanquin at the earliest point, Cuicui climbed the pagoda out back and looked over from above. Soon the wedding procession arrived: two men playing *suona*s, four strong peasant lads carrying an empty palanquin to collect the bride, a young man decked out in new clothes, who looked to be the son of a militia cap-tain, two sheep and a young boy leading them, a vat of wine, a box of glutinous rice cakes, and a gift-bearer. When the troop boarded the ferryboat, Cuicui and her grandpa joined them. Grandpa tugged the boat line, while Cuicui stood by the ornately decorated bridal sedan chair, taking note of all the faces in the procession and the tassels on the palanquin. When they got to shore, the one who looked like the militia captain's son drew a red envelope with money in it from his embroidered waist pouch and gave it to the old ferryman. That was the custom in this locality, so Grandpa could not refuse the gift. But having the money in hand, Grandpa asked the man where the bride was from, her family name, and how old she was. When he had all this information and the *suona* players began their haunting melodies again after landing, the file of men crossed over the hill and went on its way. Grandpa and Cuicui remained in the boat, their emotions following the sounds of the *suona*s far into the distance.

Weighing the red money packet in his hand, Grandpa said, "Cuicui, the bride is from the Song Family Stockade and she's only fourteen."

Cuicui understood his meaning, but paid him no heed. She began quietly to pull the boat across.

When they reached the side where their house was, Cuicui rushed home to get their little twin-pipe bamboo *suona*. She asked Grandpa to play her the tune "The Mother Sees Her Daughter Off to Marriage." She lay down with the yellow dog in a shady spot on the bluffs in front of the house, where she could watch the clouds in the sky. The days were getting longer now. Before anyone noticed, Grandpa fell asleep. So did Cuicui and the yellow dog.

CHAPTER SEVEN

It was the day of the festival. Grandpa and Cuicui had already decided three days before that he would tend the boat while Cuicui and the yellow dog would visit Shunshun's stilt house to enjoy the excitement. Cuicui hadn't agreed at first, but later she came around. Yet, a day later, Cuicui changed her mind again, insisting that they must both go to the races or stay with the ferryboat. The ferryman understood; she was at war with herself, torn between her own desire for fun and her love of him. But it wouldn't do at all if she missed the fun that was her due just because she was tethered to him! Grandpa said, with a smile, "Cuicui, what's wrong? Going back on your word is not what one expects of a Chadong girl. We stick to our promises, we don't give in to second thoughts. My memory's not so bad that I forget your promises to me as soon as you make them!" So he said, but Grandpa obviously was prone to see things however she saw them. Yet because he doted on her, her change of heart saddened him, too. Seeing her grandpa fall silent, Cuicui asked him, "If I go, who will stay with you?"

"If you go," he said, "the boat will stay with me!"

Cuicui knitted her brows and gave him a wry smile: "Oh, so the boat will look after you. Is that right?"

Grandpa thought to himself, "You *will* leave me, one day." But he didn't dare bring that up. Grandpa didn't know what to say next, so he went out back of the house to the garden beneath the pagoda and checked on the scallions. Cuicui followed.

"Grandfather, I've made my decision. I'm not going. If someone has to go, let it be the boat. I'll take its place and keep you company!"

"Cuicui, if you won't go then I will, with red flowers in my hair, made up like an old country lady going to town on her first trip!"

The two of them laughed at this for the longest time. They left the dispute open to settlement.

While Grandpa tended his scallions, Cuicui plucked a scallion with a big stem to use as a whistle. People on the east bank called out to be ferried across. Cuicui hurried over, blocking her grandpa's way. She jumped into the boat and tugged it along the cable to the other side where the passengers were. She yelled out to her grandpa:

"Sing for us, Grandfather, sing!"

But he didn't. He just stood on the high crag, watching Cuicui and waving at her silently.

Grandpa was a little worried.

Cuicui was growing up, given to blushing now when certain things inadvertently came up in conversation. The passage of time was ripening her, as if urging her forward, making her pay attention to new things. She loved now to look at brides with their powder and makeup, to adorn her own hair with wildflowers, and to listen to songs. She was beginning to understand some of the sentiments in the local Chadong love songs. She seemed a little distant sometimes; she liked to sit on the rocky bluffs, fixing her gaze on a patch of clouds or a star in the sky. Grandpa would ask, "Cuicui, what are you thinking about?" And she would whisper, embarrassed, "Cuicui's not thinking about anything." But at the same time she was asking herself, "Cuicui, what *are* you thinking about?" And she'd answer, "I'm thinking about lots of things, things that carry me far away. But I don't know what they are." She was indeed wrapped up in thought, in thought that even she could not identify. Her girl's body had now completely filled out, and she had reached the age when she experienced a miracle of nature each month. This set her to thinking all the more.

Grandpa understood the impact of such things on a girl, and this in turn affected him. He had lived his full seventy years amid nature, but some natural happenings in human life were beyond his control. Cuicui's maturation made her grandpa recall events in the past. From stories buried in the accumulations of time, certain things came back to haunt him.

Cuicui's mother had once been just like her: long eyebrows, big eyes, rosy complexion, and a winsome charm that made you adore her. She was a clever one, knowing just how to roll her eyes and arch her eyebrows to the delight of family elders. One would have thought she, too, was incapable of leaving the old man. But then misfortune came: she met the soldier. In the end, she abandoned her elder and her young one to die with that soldier. The old ferryman did not blame anyone for these things; he chalked it all up to Heaven. Cuicui's grandpa never cursed Heaven, but in his heart he could never completely accept its cruel disposition of things. He was still young at heart. He said he had put it aside, yet it was something that couldn't be put aside, even though he must.

And then there was Cuicui. If Cuicui did as her mother did, could a man of his age bring up another baby? The gods would not necessarily consent, even if he were willing! He was too old, ready for his rest. All the toil and hardship that accompanied the life of a good and honest Chinese country fellow, he had already experienced. If there really was a God up on high, and this God had two hands that could dispose of everything with perfect justice, He ought to take Grandpa first, letting the young people enjoy all that was due them in their new lives.

But Grandpa didn't think this way. He was concerned

about Cuicui. Sometimes he lay down on the bluffs under the stars to mull things over. He felt that death would be coming for him soon. The fact that Cuicui had grown up proved how old he was. Yet, whatever happened, he must get Cuicui settled. Cuicui's poor mother had given her to him. Now that she had grown up, he must pass her on to someone else before his work on earth was done! But who was the proper husband for her? Who could he be sure would never hurt her?

A few days before, when the frank and outspoken Tianbao, Shunshun's No. 1, had crossed the stream and talked to Grandpa, the first words out of his mouth were:

"Elder Uncle, your Cuicui has grown quite beautiful. She's a real Guan Yin. Two years from now, if I can take charge of business in Chadong instead of having to fly over the landscape all day like a crow, I'll be coming by this stream every night to sing to Cuicui of my love."

Grandpa smiled to encourage him to go on with this declaration. He looked at No. 1 with narrowed eyes while tugging the boat, as if to say,

"I catch the meaning of your foolish confession, and it doesn't anger me. Go on—what else have you to say?"

Whereupon No. 1 continued:

"Cuicui is so delicate, I worry that she may be suited to listening to our Chadong love songs but not the humdrum errands of an ordinary Chadong wife. I want a sweetheart who can listen to my songs but she also has to be a wife who can manage household affairs. 'I want a horse I don't have to feed, but I want it to run fast, too!' The ancestors must have thought up that saying just for me, to show that you have to feed a horse to make it run fast!"

Grandpa unhurriedly turned the boat around, putting the stern in to shore, and said:

"No. 1, anything can happen! Wait and see."

After the young man left, Grandpa mulled over the boy's frank words. He was happy and at the same time worried. Cuicui had to be entrusted to a husband. Was this the best one to take care of her? And if he did bequeath her to him, would Cuicui be willing?

CHAPTER EIGHT

A fine rain was falling at daybreak on the fifth of the month. Rising water levels upstream had provided the seasonal "Dragon Boat tide" and the river was already pea-green. Grandpa was on his way to town to buy goods for the festival, with a coolie hat made of phrynium fiber on his head and a bag containing a string of six hundred old imperial copper coins slung across his shoulder. He carried a basket and a big gourd full of wine. Because it was a festival day, folk from all the little villages and Miao stockades had come bearing goods and money for buying, selling, and trading. They had all arisen very early too, so Cuicui and the yellow dog tended the ferryboat in Grandpa's absence. Cuicui wore a brand-new coolie hat as she ferried passengers back and forth, one trip after another. To the amusement of all, the yellow dog sat in the bow and, when they landed, jumped ashore before everyone else, carrying the tie rope in his mouth. Some country folk brought their own dogs with them to town, but as the old saying goes, "dogs ought to be kept at home." Away from their territory, even accompanied by their masters, these dogs had to be on their best behavior. On the ferry, Cuicui's dog would go up and sniff at them until Cuicui threw him a cross look; he seemed to understand that she was telling him to stand back. Even after landing, when he'd done his duty with the rope, he had to follow the unfamiliar dogs all the way up the hill. Whether he was barking softly at a dog's master or following the dog, Cuicui would yell at him, with a little anger in her voice: "Hey, there, dog! What's gotten into you? What makes you run off when we have work to do?" The yellow dog would quickly run back to the boat and go back to sniffing every place in sight. Cuicui said, "What nonsense is this? Where'd you learn that? Lie down over there!" As if he understood her words, the dog immediately went to his place in the boat and only occasionally gave a few soft yaps, as if he'd just remembered something.

The rain would not let up. The river was covered with mist. When work quieted down on the boat, Cuicui rehearsed the old ferryman's itinerary in her imagination. She knew just where he was going, whom he would run into and what they would say to each other, what would be going on at the city gate and on River Street—it was all in "the ledger of her mind," as clear as if she had seen it with her own eyes. And she knew her grandpa backward and forward. Every time he met an army friend from the city, even a horse groomer or a cook boy, he would give him the proper greetings of the day. He'd say, "Honorable Soldier, may you have your fill of good food and drink this holiday!" And the other would say, "Oarsman, may you have the same!" But if the reply to this salute was "What good food and drink do you mean? Four ounces of pork and two bowls of wine are not enough to satisfy anyone or get them drunk!," Grandpa would earnestly invite his friend to Green Creek Hill to drink up. If the man wanted to drink a swig of wine from Grandpa's gourd, the ferryman would not be tightfisted—he'd hand it right over. And if the man from the garrison rolled his tongue and licked his lips while praising the wine's quality, Grandpa would press him to take another swallow. Thus was the wine dissipated, until the ferryman ran back to the shop where he'd bought it to fill his gourd up to the top again. Cuicui knew, too, that Grandpa would go to the docks to talk to sailors whose boats had put in a day or two earlier. He'd ask them the price of rice and salt downriver, and sometimes he'd stoop over and crawl into their cabins, which were steeped in the smells of squid and fish, sundry oils, vinegar, and smoke from the burning of wood. The boatmen would grab a handful of red dates from a little jar and press them on the old ferryman. When Grandpa got home and heard Cuicui's complaints about his absence, these dates became the instruments of their reconciliation. And when Grandpa got to River Street, many a shop owner would give him *zongzi* and other treats out of respect for this oarsman who was so true to his duty. Though Grandpa would shout, "It'll crush my old bones to bring back a pile this big," he always had to give in to their gestures of gratitude. He'd go to the long table where meat was sold and ask to buy, but they wouldn't take his money. If one butcher would refuse payment, he'd have to go to another rather than take advantage of others' goodwill. The butcher would say, "Elder, why are you so unyielding about this? Nobody's asking you to be a beast of burden in front of the plow!" But he wouldn't take the offering. To him, this was akin to blood money, in a class of its own. If his money wasn't accepted, he'd figure out the meat's cost, thrust the coins into the bamboo tube that was the merchant's money box, seize the purchase, and leave. The butcher, knowing how he would react beforehand, would give Grandpa the choicest portion and make sure it was overweight. But the ferryman might notice that and say, "Hey there, boss, I don't want any favors! Tenderloin cuts are for city people to sauté with squid. Don't make me laugh! I want meat from the neck, rich and sticky. I row a boat. I want to make a stew of it with carrots while I drink my wine!" Meat in hand, he'd count out his payment before handing it over, then insist that the butcher count it again, but the latter would ignore this and throw the coins carelessly into his money tube. The ferryman, as he left, would give a smile that had to be called ingratiating. The butcher and his other customers found this hilarious.

Cuicui knew, too, that Grandpa would go to Shunshun's house on River Street.

She mused about everything she had seen and heard on the festival days of the past two years, joyful at heart, as if something had come to her, like the elusive yellow sunflower she saw with her eyes closed as she lay in bed in the morning. This thing loomed bright and bold before her, but she couldn't see it clearly or quite grasp it.

Cuicui wondered: "Are there really tigers at White Rooster Pass?" She had no idea why she suddenly remembered White Rooster Pass. It was located in the middle reaches of the You River, over seventy miles from Chadong!

And then she thought: "Thirty-two men hefting six heavy oars, hoisting a great sail when the wind comes up, made from one hundred lengths of white cloth, crossing Lake Dongting in such a giant boat—how absurd!" She had no idea how big Lake Dongting was, nor had she ever seen such a big boat. Even funnier, she couldn't herself imagine why these thoughts had come to her.

A group arrived to be ferried across, people with goods: men who looked like government messengers and a mother and daughter. The mother wore a blue outfit that had been starched stiff as a board and the girl's cheeks were rouged like two round cakes. She wore new clothes that didn't fit too well. They were going to town to greet their relatives at the festival and see the dragon boats. After waiting for the group to get settled on the boat, Cuicui gave the girl a once-over while she pulled the boat across the stream. To Cuicui, the girl looked to be about eleven and already very spoiled, always hanging on to her mother. Her newly polished shoes had pointy toes and spikes on the bottom, but they were splashed with mud. Her trousers were made of leek-green cotton cloth with specks of purple. When she saw Cuicui staring at her, she stared back with eyes bright as crystal balls. She looked a little embarrassed, ill at ease, and at the same time indefinably seductive. The mother then asked Cuicui how old she was. Cuicui smiled, unwilling to answer, and instead asked how old her daughter was. When she said twelve years old, Cuicui couldn't suppress a laugh. They were obviously the wife and daughter of a rich man; one could tell from their manner. Cuicui spotted a pair of bracelets on the girl, made of interlaced strands of silver. They flashed a shiny white light and made Cuicui feel a little envious. When the boat reached shore and everyone was off, the woman took out a copper coin and pressed it into Cuicui's hand before going. Forgetting her grandpa's rule for the moment, Cuicui neither thanked her nor gave it back. She just gaped from behind at the girl among the file of people. The group was about to go up the hill when Cuicui suddenly chased after them. At the top of the hill, she returned the money to the woman, who said, "It's for you!" Cuicui just smiled and shook her head without replying, to indicate that she couldn't accept it, and without waiting for the woman to say another word, she quickly ran back to her ferryboat.

When she reached the boat, people on the opposite shore were summoning the ferry, so Cuicui tugged the boat across. Seven people crossed on this trip, among them two more girls, who also wore clean outfits to go see the boat races. But they were not so attractive; this made Cuicui fix her mind all the more on the previous girl.

More people than usual needed ferrying today, especially girls. Cuicui pulled them across on the boat, so they made a deep impression on her: the pretty ones, the funny-looking ones, the nice ones, ones with reddened eyes. When the crowds stopped, while she waited for Grandpa and Grandpa didn't come, she reviewed all of the girls in her mind and sang softly and distractedly:

> *The tiger at White Rooster Pass feasts on people*
> *And he'll get the militia captain's daughter first.*
> *Sister No. 1 wears a pair of gold hairpins,*
> *Sister No. 2, a pair of silver bracelets,*
> *But Sister No. 3, little me, has no jewelry to be*
> *   found;*
> *Just bean-sprout earrings, worn all the year round.*

A man came from town who'd seen the old ferryman in front of a tavern on River Street, offering a young boatman his gourd full of freshly bought white liquor. Cuicui inquired further and he told all. She laughed to hear of her grandpa's generosity, offered at just the wrong time and the wrong place. As the man departed, Cuicui again began to softly hum, just for fun, the chant that the local shaman used to summon the gods:

> *Gods and immortals, open your eyes and look at us*
>   *down here!*
> *Our young are honest and healthy.*
> *Our elders know how to drink, and work, and sleep;*
> *Our children grow up to withstand hunger and cold;*
> *Our oxen are willing to plow, our sheep to birth, our*
>   *fowl to hatch eggs;*
> *Our women are good at raising children, singing, and*
>   *finding their true loves!*
> *Gods and immortals, come on down and have a look.*
> *Lord Guan, mount the Red-haired Steed,*
> *General Weichi Gong, brandish the iron whip.*
> *Gods and immortals above, ride down on the clouds*
>   *and look around!*
> *Old Man Zhang Guo, ride steady on your donkey,*
> *Iron Crutch Li, be careful where you step!*
>
> *Riches and emoluments without end come from the*
>   *gods;*

Timely winds and rains, too, come from your favor,
So good wine and food are laid before you,
Fat pigs and sheep are frying in the pan.

Hong Xiuquan, Li Hongzhang,
Once you were lords of all around,
Murder and arson—suicide and loyalty—each has
　　its art,
So join the feast, it's for you to take part.

Eat and drink, please take your time,
Moon's up and breeze's down; fording the river will
　　be just fine.
If you're drunk I'll take your hand and lead you
　　along,
So I can treat you to another song.

The melody was very sweet, full of happiness tinged with melancholy. When she finished singing it, Cuicui felt a little despondent. She recalled the prairie fires and drumbeats at the end of autumn when it was time for rewarding the gods and redeeming promises to them.

The drumbeats from afar had already begun to sound. She knew that this must mark the dragon boats, painted with their vermilion stripes, going into the river. It was still drizzling endlessly and a layer of mist hung over the creek.

CHAPTER NINE

When Grandpa got home, it was almost time for breakfast. Arms and shoulder poles laden with packages, he called out for Cuicui from the top of the hill for her to pull the boat across the stream to meet him. Having seen so many people getting to go to town, Cuicui there in the boat was beside herself with impatience, but the sound of her grandpa picked up her spirits. She hollered back, shrilly, "Grandfather, Grandfather, I'm coming!" When the old ferryman had got into the boat and set down his load in the prow, he helped tug the boat as he smiled at Cuicui, himself as meek and bashful as a child. "Cuicui, I'll bet you thought I was never coming, didn't you?" She was going to complain to her grandpa, but instead she answered, "Grandfather, I knew you were on River Street, plying people with wine, having a wonderful time." Cuicui knew how much her grandpa loved to hang around on River Street, but to go on about it would have made her grandpa sputter embarrassed denials, so she kept it back.

Counting up all the bundles in the prow, Cuicui noticed that the wine gourd was missing. She snickered.

"Grandfather, you're so generous, letting all those soldiers and boatmen drink off you, you even let them swallow your gourd!"

Smiling, Grandpa quickly put in:

"No way, no way. Elder Brother Shunshun took it away from me. He saw me out on River Street inviting people to have a drink and said, 'Hey there, Captain Zhang Heng of the ferrymen, we can't have this. You don't own a distillery! How can you go on like this? If you have to be a philanthropist, a real sport like the heroes of Mount Liang, then give it over, I'll drink it up for you!' That's what he said, 'I'll drink it up for you!' I put down my wine gourd. But I figure he was kidding me. Is there any lack of wine in his household? What do you think, Cuicui?"

"Grandfather, do you really think it was about him having a drink, even if it was all in jest?"

"What, then?"

"Nothing to be upset over, he must have confiscated your gourd because you picked the wrong place to be serving all comers; he didn't want you to end up with no liquor at all. He'll send it back with one of his men in a little while. You still don't get it! For Heaven's sake!"

"Do you really think he will?"

By this time the boat had reached the shore. Cuicui hurried to help her grandpa gather up his bundles before he could pick them up, but all she got was a lone fish and the embroidered waist pouch. The money was already gone; in its place were a packet of white sugar and a box of sesame cakes.

The two had just brought the new purchases into the house when someone hailed them for service from the other side of the stream. Asking Cuicui to keep an eye on the meat and vegetables lest a feral cat get them, Grandpa rushed ahead of her to the ferry. After a short time, he headed back home with the passenger, speaking loudly and excitedly. The visitor had indeed come to return the gourd. Grandpa said, "Cuicui, you guessed right! He really did bring it back!"

Before Cuicui could escape into the kitchen, Grandpa entered the house with a young man. He was dark and broad-shouldered.

Cuicui and the visitor smiled at each other, letting Grandpa talk on. The guest kept on looking and smiling at Cuicui, who seemed to realize what the staring meant. She began to grow a little embarrassed, so she went into the kitchen to light the fire in the stove. When yet another person came to the stream and hailed the ferry, she ran out the door to the boat and took him across. And just then there was another passenger. Though it was drizzling, there were far more people to serve than usual, requiring three trips. Once on board, as

Cuicui tended the boat, she began thinking about her grand-dad's happy mood. She sensed, somehow, that she knew this city fellow who'd been dispatched to return the wine gourd. But though he looked familiar, she didn't know where she'd seen him before. She seemed unwilling to figure it all out and could not guess his identity.

Grandpa hollered from the bluff: "Cuicui! Cuicui! Come up and sit awhile, keep our guest company!" She'd intended to go ashore and light the stove since no one needed ferrying, but now that her grandpa had called her, she didn't.

The visitor asked Grandpa, "Are you going to town to see the boats?" "I have to stay with my boat," replied the old ferry-man. The two continued talking about other things. Finally, the visitor came to the point:

"Uncle, your Cuicui is grown up now. She's very pretty!"

The ferryman smiled. "He talks just like his elder brother—says exactly what's on his mind," he thought to himself. But he said, "No. 2, you're the only one in these parts who deserves that praise. Everybody says you're hand-some! Folks have made up epithets to acclaim your virtues: the Leopard of Bamian Mountain, the Golden Pheasant of Didi Stream!"

"What nonsense!"

"They've really captured you! I heard some boatmen say that last time when you were piloting a boat and it wrecked up below the Three Gorges in the rapids at White Rooster

Pass, you rescued three men from the dashing waves. They say you stayed overnight by the rapids, and when the village girls got a look at you, they crooned the night away with love songs outside your shack. Is it true?"

"That wasn't any serenading by young women, that was the howling of wolves! The place is famous for them, just looking for the chance to eat us! We kept a big campfire to scare them off—that's the only way we escaped with our lives!"

The old ferryman chuckled: "All the more! What they said about you was right! A wolf only picks out young maidens and children to eat—and handsome young seventeen-year-olds—never an old bones like me. It'd take one sniff at me and go away!"

At that, No. 2 said, "Uncle, you've seen a lot of sunrises in this locale. Everybody says the excellent feng shui here, the geomancy, is propitious for the emergence of great men. I wonder why we haven't had one so far?"

"You mean the good feng shui should have given us someone with a big name? I don't see anything so bad about not having such a person born in a little place like this. It's enough that we have young people who are bright, honest, brave, and able to work hard. The men in your family, for instance, have brought this place a lot of glory!"

"Uncle, you're right, I was just thinking that. This place of ours produces good men, not bad men—men like you, Uncle. You may be old, but you're still as strong as a nanmu tree, living a steady and stable life on this patch of earth— both decent and generous. There aren't many like you."

"I'm an old man, what am I worth? I've had everything that was my lot in life: sun and rain, long journeys bearing heavy loads, living it up on food and liquor, then suffering hunger and cold—and pretty soon, I'll be lying beneath the cold, cold earth, feeding the earthworms. There's plenty waiting on this earth for you young folk. If you do your work well, it won't let you down—just hold up your end of the bargain."

"Uncle, with your diligence setting the example, we young people dare not let you down!"

They'd been talking for some time, so No. 2 was ready to go. The old ferryman stood outside his doorway and called for Cuicui to come into the house to boil water and cook a meal while he took her place on the boat. Cuicui didn't want to come ashore, but the guest had already boarded the boat, so as she tugged the boat, Grandpa pretended to scold her:

"Cuicui, aren't you coming back? Surely you don't expect me to be a housewife and do the cooking?"

Throwing a sidelong glance at the visitor, Cuicui saw that he was staring at her. Turning her head away and pursing her lips, she smartly attended to her business pulling on the cable, until she'd slowly pulled the boat onto the shore. The visitor stood in the prow and said to Cuicui,

"Cuicui, when you've eaten, won't you come with your grandfather to our stilt house and watch the boat race?"

At first too embarrassed to speak, Cuicui finally answered, "Grandfather says he's not going, because then there'd be no one to tend the ferry!"

"Won't you come?"

"If Grandfather won't go, neither will I."

"Do you have to tend the boat, too?"

"I want to be with Grandfather."

"What if I get someone to take your place on the boat?"

The boat reached the shore with a thud as it bumped into a mound of earth. No. 2 jumped up on the bank and said, from the slope:

"Cuicui, I've put you to trouble. When I get home, I'll send someone to take the place of both of you. Eat your meal and hurry on over to my house to see the boats. A lot of people are there already, it's very lively!"

Misunderstanding the good intentions of this stranger, and why she had to go to his house to see the boats, Cuicui giggled between her little pursed lips and pulled the boat back to the other shore. When she got to the bank where her home was, the young man had reached the top of the hill on the other side. He was still there, as if waiting for something. Cuicui went home and lit the fire. She stuffed some damp grasses into the stove and inquired of her grandpa, who was just then testing out the wine in the gourd returned by the visitor.

"Grandfather, that fellow said he was going back to get

someone to replace you, so the two of us can go see the races. Will you go?"

"Would you like to?"

"If we go together. I like that young man. He seems familiar. Who is he?"

"Good, he likes you, too!" Grandpa thought to himself. He said, with a smile, "Cuicui, don't you remember two years ago, you were on the big riverbank and someone said you might be eaten by a big fish?"

Cuicui understood, but she pretended not to. She asked, "Who is he, then?"

"Think, Cuicui. Take a guess."

"I couldn't possibly guess who he is."

"He's No. 2 of Fleetmaster Shunshun's household. He remembered you, but you still don't remember him!" He took a sip of wine and said, in a low voice, as if to praise the wine and a certain man at the same time: "Good, just right. You're not this lucky very often!"

People wanting the ferry hailed him from outside the door. The old grandpa reiterated, "Good, just right . . ." Then in a flash he was in the boat, getting down to work.

CHAPTER TEN

While they were eating, someone called for the ferry on the far bank. Cuicui rushed to the boat. When she got to the other shore, she saw that her passenger was the boatman sent by Fleetmaster Shunshun to take their place. He looked at Cuicui and said, "No. 2 wants you to come over when you finish eating. He's already in his dragon boat." He said the same thing when he saw Grandpa.

Straining their ears, they could hear the faraway drumbeats picking up their pace, and from that they could picture the very slender boats dashing straight ahead across the Long Depths, their wakes leaving long and exquisitely beautiful lines in the water.

Unwilling even to stop for tea, the newcomer took a position in the prow of the boat. Cuicui and Grandpa had invited him in during their meal, but he shook his head. Grandpa said,

"Cuicui, I'm not going, why don't you and the little dog go on without me?"

"If you don't go, I don't want to, either!"

"And if I do?"

"I didn't really want to, but I'd go with you."

Grandpa smiled: "All right, Cuicui, you come with me, keep me company!"

❧

By the time Grandpa and Cuicui got to the big river in the city, the banks had been crowded with spectators for some time. The drizzle had stopped, but the ground was still wet. Grandpa wanted Cuicui to go to the fleetmaster's stilt house on River Street to watch the races, but something seemed to be weighing on her mind that made her afraid to go there; she preferred to stand by the riverbank. Though the two stayed in place there, it wasn't long before Shunshun sent someone to invite them in. His house on stilts was already crowded. The upper-class country mother and daughter that had caught Cuicui's eye when she ferried them that morning occupied the two best seats in the house, by the window. The daughter spotted Cuicui and said: "Come here, over here!" Cuicui went over, a little self-consciously, and sat on a bench behind them. Grandpa set off.

Instead of watching the dragon boats race, Grandpa let an acquaintance lead him away to see the new grain mill and its water-powered stone roller a quarter-mile upstream. The old ferryman happened to be intensely interested in that mill. In a tiny thatched hut nestled between the mountain and the river was the round millstone, fixed vertically on a horizontal axle and resting at a tilt on top of a circular pathway of crushed stone along which it would make its revolutions. When the sluice gate was pulled up, water rushed down upon a concealed underground wheel, and the round millstone up above flew into action, rotating on its axle as it made its rounds over the circular pathway under it. The miller poured his unhusked rice into the groove of the stone circuit on the bottom. When the polished rice came out, he sifted away the powdery chaff in a rectangular bamboo sieve basket he kept in the corner of the hut. The floor was covered in this dust from the chaff, and so were the miller's head and shoulders, from top to bottom, including the white cloth he wrapped around his head like a turban. In good weather he went out to the open spaces around the millhouse, where he planted turnips, cabbages, garlic, and scallions. When the millrace got damaged, he took off his trousers and went into the river to pile up rocks so as to plug the leak. Once his dikes were firmly built, he could build a net of branches across the millrace, like a bridge. When the waters rose, fish would swim right over the dike into it, without the miller's having to lift a finger! Compared to running a ferry, running a mill was a more multifaceted and interesting job; that was clear at a glance.

But it was wholly in vain for a ferryman to hope to have a mill someday. Mills all belonged to the local rich people. The old ferryman's friend told him who the mill's owner was. The two men looked over every corner of it as they chatted.

The ferryman's friend kicked the new millstone and said:

"The people of Middle Stockade live up high in the mountains, but they like to buy property down here by the river; this mill belongs to Middle Stockade's Militia Captain Wang. Cost him seven hundred strings of cash, a thousand coppers to a string!"

The old ferryman rolled his small eyes and nodded, sizing up everything enviously and appreciatively, even offering fitting criticisms of every constituent part. Then the two men took a seat on a still-unfinished bench. The friend went on about this mill's future—it probably would be the dowry of the militia captain's daughter. Then he thought of Cuicui, and remembered something that Shunshun's No. 1 had asked him to do for him. He inquired,

"Uncle, how old is Cuicui now?"

"Thirteen, going on fourteen." Having said this, the old ferryman continued counting up the years and months to himself.

"What a clever girl for a thirteen-year-old! Whoever gets matched to her will be a lucky fellow!"

"How so? She doesn't have any such mill for a dowry. She'll go empty-handed."

"Don't call her that, she's a hard worker. Her two hands are worth more than five mills! Lu Ban built the bridge at Luoyang with his two hands! . . ." He went on, trying to refute the old ferryman, until he laughed at his own words.

The old ferryman laughed too, thinking to himself: "Cuicui has two hands all right, but if she built a Luoyang Bridge, that would be a first!"

The other man paused and then said:

"Young men here in Chadong have good eyes and they're very good at picking their wives. Uncle, if it wouldn't offend you, I'd like to tell you a funny little story."

"What funny story?" asked the old ferryman.

The other said, "Uncle, don't be upset with me, but you can take this one seriously, if you want."

He went on to say how No. 1 in Shunshun's family had praised Cuicui and sent him on an errand of inquiring about the old ferryman's opinion. Finally he related another conversation he'd had. "I asked him, 'No. 1, are you in earnest or are you playing with me?' He replied, 'Go sound out the old man for me, will you? I'm sweet on Cuicui, I long for her! I mean it!' So I said, 'I'm very blunt in expressing myself, and once I speak, I can't take it back—just suppose, what if the old man slaps me one?' He said, 'If you're afraid of his reaction, tell it first as something humorous. That'll save you from any beating!' So you see, Uncle, this funny story I told you is about something real. Think it over. When he comes to see me after he returns from Eastern Sichuan on the ninth of the month, what should I tell him?"

The old ferryman recalled what No. 1 had said in his own words during his last visit. He knew that No. 1 had spoken frankly, and also that Shunshun liked Cuicui, so he was elated. But local custom said that No. 1 would have to come in person with gifts of cakes to Green Creek Hill and speak for himself to prove his seriousness. The old ferryman said, "When he gets home, you tell him that after hearing your funny story, the old codger told one of his own—'In a game of chess, the chariot—the rook—moves one way and the horse-man—the knight—another. If No. 1 wants to make his move directly like a chariot, his father ought to ask a go-between and put the proposition to me in the proper way. If he wants to move like a horseman, hurdling all obstacles, it's his play, to stand on the bluffs across the creek from the ferry and sing for Cuicui's heart until he's won her—for "three years and six months," if that's what it takes, as it says in the song.'"

"Uncle, if singing to her for three years and six months can move her heart, I'll start tomorrow and try to win her myself!"

"If Cuicui were willing, do you think I could refuse?"

"That's not it. People think that if you make the decision, Cuicui can't object."

"That's not right. This is about her!"

"Even if it is, the elder has to have the final say. People

will still think that singing three years and six months, be it under sunlight or moonlight, is less important than a good word from you!"

"In that case, let's do it this way. When he returns home from Sichuan, have him talk it over with Shunshun. Meanwhile, I'll ask Cuicui. If she prefers to follow a man who's sung for her three years and six months, I'll have to ask you to persuade No. 1 to choose that zigzag horseman's move."

"Fine. When I see him, I'll say: 'No. 1, I told him the words in jest. As to the words in truth, that will depend on your fate.' And so it will be, but I know that his fate still lies tightly within your grasp, old fellow."

"That's not true! If it were within my grasp to decide this matter, I'd agree right away!"

With that settled, the two went to see a new, three-cabin boat that Shunshun had just purchased. Meanwhile, things had been going on in Shunshun's stilt house along River Street.

Cuicui had gone to sit near the daughter of the rich folk from the countryside. Her location was spectacular; everything out on the river was clearly visible from the window, but Cuicui felt a little ill at ease. The people who crowded around the other windows to see the excitement all seemed frequently to divert their gaze from the river to Cuicui and her company. Some even pretended to have some reason for passing by, when in fact they were just interested in sizing up these people Cuicui was sitting with. Cuicui felt uneasy. She just wanted an excuse to run away. Soon a cannon sounded out on the river and several boats that had assembled on the farther shore rowed straight toward them. Four boats took the lead in close formation, like four arrows shooting evenly through the water. Halfway across, two had already gone ahead of the others, and a little later, one of those pulled into the lead. As the spectators saw it reach the customs house, another cannon shot announced the victory. One could begin to make out that the winning boat was the one belonging to River Street. Congratulatory firecrackers were heard all around. The victors rowed past the stilt houses of River Street, their drum pounding as crowds along the streets and in the dangling foot houses shouted out joyous congratulations. Cuicui noticed that the red-turbaned young man standing firmly in the prow, brandishing the little flag that gave the crew directions, was none other than No. 2—the one who had returned the gourd of wine to Green Creek Hill. Her mind flashed back to events two years earlier. "A big fish might eat you!" "Whether it eats me or not, it's no concern of yours!" "All right, I won't worry about it!" "Hey, dog, save your barks for those who are worth it!" At that, Cuicui remembered the yellow dog that had come with her. She'd long since lost him, so she got up from her place and searched all over the house, completely forgetting the young man in the prow of the boat.

As she looked for her dog in the crowd, she overheard some conversations.

A woman with a broad face asked, "Whose family is she from, to get that prime seat in front of a window at Shunshun's house?"

Another woman responded, "She's the daughter of the country gentleman Wang up in one of the stockades. They say they came to see the boats, but really they're here to look over people—and be looked at! They must be something, to merit such a good place!"

"Who's come to look at whom?"

"Goodness, don't you know—that country gentleman wants his daughter to marry into Shunshun's family."

"Who might they want to betroth to her? No. 1 or No. 2?"

"No. 2. Just wait, and we'll see this Yue Yun come up and pay respects to his future mother-in-law!"

Another woman cut in: "The match is made, and it's a good one! The girl brings as dowry a brand-new mill by the river, which can do the work of ten hired laborers."

Someone asked, "What does No. 2 think about that?"

Yet another person whispered, "No. 2 said, 'I don't need to look at her. To start with, I don't want to be a miller!'"

"Did you hear Yue Yun say that?"

"That's what someone told me. They also said that No. 2 likes that girl at the ferry."

"He's no dummy; if he doesn't want to be a miller, would he really want to be a ferryman?"

"Who knows? Anyway, as the saying goes, 'People eat

what they like, even beef with chives.' A ferryboat needn't be any worse than a grain mill!"

They were all looking at the river as they gossiped, so no one noticed that Cuicui was right behind them.

Cuicui went away, her face burning with embarrassment, only to hear another pair of women talking about these same things. "Everything is settled. They're just waiting for No. 2 to give the word." And, "Just from the spirit that No. 2 showed in today's race, you could almost guess that he got it from a young maiden watching him from onshore!"

Who was this young maiden who so moved No. 2?

Cuicui was too short to see over the people and take in the river scenes now. It was only from the swelling of the drumbeats as they drew nearer and more frantic, and the rise in hubbub from the crowd onshore, that she realized that No. 2's boat had rowed up to the house. People upstairs in the house were cheering, too, and calling out No. 2's name; over by the rich lady from the countryside, they were setting off strings of hundred-pop firecrackers. Suddenly there arose other shouts, of astonishment and dismay, as a crowd of people went out the door to go down to the river. Not knowing what had gone wrong, Cuicui felt a little confused. She didn't know whether to go back to her original seat or keep standing in back of the spectators. But just then a tray full of *zongzi* and fine cakes was set before the rich country lady and her little miss, so Cuicui felt uncomfortable going back there. She decided to squeeze out the door and see what was going on by the river. A passageway next to a salt company led from River Street down to the water, under overhanging beams and rafters. She emerged head-on into a crowd of people swarming around No. 2 in his red turban. He had slipped and fallen into the water, but made his way out on his own. Cuicui dodged to get out of the way, but the path was so narrow that she still found herself elbow-to-elbow with the oncoming surge of people. No. 2 spotted Cuicui and said,

"Cuicui, you came! Did your grandfather come, too?"

Her face flushed crimson, Cuicui was too embarrassed to speak. She thought to herself, "Where has my yellow dog run off to?"

No. 2 continued:

"Why not go up to my house to watch the proceedings? I told them to save you a good seat."

Cuicui thought to herself: "A mill for a dowry—how fine is that?"

No. 2 couldn't persuade Cuicui to go back, so they went their separate ways. When she got to the river, her young heart was filled with feelings she could not understand. Was she annoyed? No! Worried? Not that, either. Happy, then? No, what would she be happy about? Angry, perhaps. Yes, that was it, she seemed to be angry at someone, and also at herself. It was so crowded there by the river. In the shallow waters by the docks, in the rigging and on the awnings of the boats, even among the support columns of the stilt houses, people were everywhere. Cuicui mumbled to herself: "Why all the commotion? Did somebody find a three-legged cat?" She had hoped to find her grandfather on one of the boats, but after checking them all, she found no sign of him. She jostled her way down to the riverbank and spotted the yellow dog enjoying the excitement with one of Shunshun's laborers in an empty boat a few yards from shore. Cuicui called him twice in a shrill voice. The yellow dog pricked up his ears and head, looking all around, before bounding into the river and swimming to Cuicui. Soaked by the time he got to her, he shook himself and jumped up and down without cease, until Cuicui shouted, "Enough! What is this craziness, dog? Your boat didn't turn over. Who asked you to jump into the water?"

Cuicui and the yellow dog looked for Grandpa everywhere. They ran into him in front of a lumber store on River Street.

The old ferryman said, "Cuicui, I've just seen a first-rate grain mill! The millstone is new and so is the waterwheel—even the roof thatching is fresh! The dam releases water in such a raging torrent that when the sluice gate is pulled up, it gets the waterwheel to spinning like a top."

"Whose mill is it?" Cuicui asked, a little affectedly.

"Whose mill? Why, Squire Wang's, who lives up in the

mountains at Middle Stockade, the militia captain. I've heard tell that it will be his daughter's dowry. Now that's extravagance for you. Building it cost them seven hundred strings of cash, not including the windmill or the furnishings!"

"Who's going to marry his daughter?"

Grandpa looked at Cuicui and forced a smile. "A big fish is going to bite you. He'll bite you."

Precisely because she knew a thing or two about this matter, Cuicui pretended not to understand. She pressed Grandpa: "Grandfather, who will get that mill?"

"No. 2, Yue Yun!" Grandpa said, also muttering to himself. "Some people envy No. 2 for getting the mill; others envy the mill for getting No. 2!"

"Who's envious, Grandfather?"

"I'm envious," Grandpa said, with a smile.

Cuicui said, "Grandfather, you're drunk."

"But No. 2 says you're very pretty."

Cuicui: "Grandfather, you're crazy."

Grandpa said, "Your grandfather is not drunk and he's not crazy. Come on, let's go down to the river and see them release the ducks. Too bad I'm too old to dive in and catch one to bring home and cook in a pot with ginger." He wanted to add: "If No. 2 catches a duck, he'll give it to us." But before he could say it, up came No. 2. He stood before Cuicui and smiled. Cuicui smiled back.

The three of them went back up to the house on stilts.

CHAPTER ELEVEN

A man arrived at Green Creek Hill bearing gifts. Dock-master Shunshun had indeed asked a matchmaker to go to the ferry to seek matrimonial relations for his first son. Flustered, the old ferryman brought him across the creek and into the house. Cuicui, who was shelling peas outside by the door, at first paid the guest little attention. But when she heard the matchmaker say, "Congratulations, congratulations," at the door, she began to worry. Unwilling to squat by the front door any longer, she pretended to be shooing away the chickens in the vegetable garden. Flailing a bamboo whistling pole in the air, she softly scolded them as she ran toward the white pagoda in back.

The visitor made small talk. When they got around to the matter at hand, namely Shunshun's initiative, the old ferryman didn't know how to respond. He could only rub his big, calloused hands together, as if he couldn't believe it. The expression on his face seemed to say: "Fine, this is wonderful," yet the old man said not a word in reply.

When the visitor finished, he asked Grandpa what he thought about it. The old ferryman smiled and nodded: "So No. 1 wants to make the chariot's move, that's just fine. But I must ask Cuicui, to get her reaction." After he had seen off the visitor, Grandpa stood in the prow of the boat and called Cuicui down to the river for a talk.

Bringing a pan of peas down with her to the stream, Cuicui boarded the boat and asked her grandpa, with all the charm she could muster, "Grandfather, what is it?" Grandpa smiled in silence. Tilting his hoary white head, he looked at Cuicui for a long time. Cuicui sat down in the boat, a little taken aback. She bent over to continue shelling her peas when she heard the call of a yellow finch from the bamboo grove. Cuicui thought: "The days are growing longer, and Grandfather is taking longer to get his words out, too." Her heart was gently pounding.

After another pause, Grandpa said: "Cuicui—Cuicui—do you know what that visit was all about?"

Cuicui answered, "No, I don't." But her face and neck flushed crimson.

Observing all this, Grandpa sensed Cuicui's anxiety and looked up far away across the sky. In the mist he saw Cuicui's mother as she was fifteen years earlier, and his heart melted. He said, under his breath, "Every boat needs a berth, and every sparrow needs a nest." He began to think about the unhappy fate of Cuicui's mother. His heart ached and he smiled with difficulty.

And Cuicui—Cuicui was thinking about so many things, amid the calls of the finches and cuckoo birds in the mountains and the chops of lumbermen felling bamboos in the valleys. Stories of tigers eating people, and the mountain songs people sang to belittle and make fun of each other, the square pit in which papermakers mixed their pulp, the molten iron that flowed out of a foundry smelting furnace—she felt compelled to recollect everything her ears had heard and her eyes had seen. It seemed to be her way of putting aside the present matter and wishing it away. And yet she misunderstood what was really going on.

Grandpa said: "Cuicui, Fleetmaster Shunshun's family invited a matchmaker to ask for you as their daughter-in-law. They sought my permission. But I'm old. I might pass from the scene a couple of years from now, so it's not fit for me to delay things. This is all about you. You think it over and you give me your decision. If you're willing, then it's settled. If not, that's all right, too."

Cuicui had no idea what to do. Pretending to be unruffled, she timidly eyed her old grandpa. She didn't feel like asking for an explanation, and certainly not like giving an answer.

Grandpa added: "No. 1 is a man of good prospects. He's

fair-minded and generous. If you marry him, you can say you're blessed with good fate!"

Cuicui understood for the first time: the intended match was with No. 1! She didn't raise her head. Her heart beat fast and her face burned as she went on shelling her peas, from time to time throwing empty pods into the creek and watching them drift slowly downstream, as if she had calmed down.

Grandpa responded to Cuicui's silence with a smile. "Cuicui, it's fine if you want to think it over for a few days. Luoyang Bridge wasn't built overnight. You've got time. When No. 1 came the time before, he spoke to me about this and I told him then: chariots have to move like chariots, and horsemen like horsemen, according to the rules. If his father was going to take charge of this, he had to have a matchmaker do it according to custom—that's how chariots move; if he wanted to take charge of it himself, he had to go up into the bamboo grove on the bluffs across the creek and sing for you, three years and six months—that's the horseman's move. If you prefer the horseman's move, I'm sure he'll sing passionate songs during the day and tender ones in the moonlight, like a nightingale, singing his throat out until he spits blood!"

Cuicui remained silent. She felt like crying, but for no apparent reason. Grandpa got to talking again, and now he came to Cuicui's dead mother. After a while, he fell silent. Dipping her head in sadness, Cuicui could see tears in her grandpa's eyes. Upset and afraid, she fearfully asked him, "Grandfather, what's the matter?" Without saying a word, Grandpa clumsily wiped his eyes with the palm of his hand. He jumped ashore and ran home, giggling like a little boy.

Upset, Cuicui couldn't bring herself to run after him.

As it cleared up after the rain, the sun beat down painfully on people's backs and shoulders. The reeds and water-willow shrubs by the creek, like the vegetables in the garden, ran riot, bearing a hint of wild vitality. Green grasshoppers flew among the thick grasses, their wings setting a stir in the wind. Newly emerged cicadas on the branches had not yet set up a din, but their noise was gradually strengthening. In the stunning verdure of the emerald bamboo groves on the mountains, yellow finches, bamboo finches, and cuckoos sang in turn. Cuicui looked and listened, took it all in, and also reflected:

"Grandfather is seventy this year . . . three years and six months—who gave us that white duck? . . . what luck to get that mill, or is the mill even luckier to get him? . . ."

In her own little world, she stood up abruptly, spilling half her pan of peas into the creek. As she retrieved the pan from the water, someone hailed the ferry from the other shore.

CHAPTER TWELVE

The next day, Cuicui was in the vegetable garden below the white pagoda again when Grandpa asked for her decision. Her heart still pounding, she bowed her head as if she hadn't heard and went on picking her scallions. Grandpa smiled and thought: "I'd better wait till later. If I keep at her, she'll pick every scallion in sight!" Yet he also sensed something strange in her manner. He couldn't very well continue in this vein, so he stifled his words and changed the subject with a contrived joke.

The weather was warming day by day. It was hot by the time the sixth month drew near. The old ferryman found time to drag a black earthenware vat covered with dust out of the corner of the house and piece together some wood slats to make a round lid for it. He also took out his saw and made a tripod stand, whittled a big bamboo tube as a ladle for dipping out tea, then tied it to the vat with kudzu vine. After he'd moved this vat out the door to the stream bank, Cuicui would boil a big pot of water every morning to make tea. Sometimes she'd add tea leaves; other times, she'd just drop in some burned crusts from their cooked rice. The old ferry- man, as was his custom, prepared native cures from roots and tree bark to heal sunstroke, stomachaches, blisters, and sores. He kept these medicines close at hand. The moment he saw a passenger who didn't look right, he'd press the traveler to try his remedies, relating the source of his many prescriptions (it went without saying that he learned them from the med- ics and spirit healers in town). Bare-armed the day long, he stood firm in his square-nosed ferryboat, often bare-headed, too, his short, white hair shining like silver in the sunlight. Cuicui acted happy, running around outside the house sing- ing. When not on the move, she sat in front of the house on the high bluffs, in the shade, playing her little bamboo flute. Grandfather acted as if he had completely forgotten No. 1's marriage proposal, so of course Cuicui did, too.

But before long the matchmaker returned to sound them out. As before, Grandpa relegated the matter to Cuicui and sent the go-between back. Later he had another talk with Cuicui, again without any resolution.

The old ferryman couldn't guess what the obstacle was, or how to fix it. He'd lie in bed, mulling it over until finally it began to occur to him that perhaps Cuicui loved the younger brother, not the elder. That made him smile, an unnatural smile from fear. In truth he was a little worried, because it suddenly occurred to him that Cuicui was like her mother in every way. He had a vague feeling that mother and daughter would share the same fate. Events of the past swarmed into his mind and he could no longer sleep. He ran out the door alone, onto the high bluffs by the creek. He looked up at the stars and listened to the katydids and sounds of the other insects, constant as rain. He could not sleep for a very long time.

Cuicui, of course, was unaware of this. A young girl whose days were always filled with play and work, she felt something very mysterious racing within her little heart, but when night came, she went peacefully to sleep.

And yet, everything changes with time. This family's quiet and ordinary life, as days came and went in succession, saw the peace in its human affairs completely broken.

In Fleetmaster Shunshun's household, Tianbao's actions were already known to No. 2, and Nuosong let his elder brother know what was on his mind, too. They were brothers in the hardships of love, both loving the granddaughter of a ferryman. This did not seem at all peculiar to the local folk. A common saying in the borderlands was: "Fire can burn and water can flow anywhere; sunshine and moonshine also reach everywhere; and so, too, does love." It was not remarkable that the sons of a rich fleetmaster had fallen in love with the granddaughter of a poor ferryman. There was one problem. Would the brothers decide who would marry the girl by the usual Chadong practice of a bloody struggle?

These brothers would never take up arms against each other, but neither were they accustomed to "yielding in the contest of love," like the laughable behavior of cowardly city males when faced with matters of love and hate.

The elder took his younger brother to a shipbuilder's yard upstream to see the family's new boat, then told the younger boy all that was in his heart, adding that his affection had been growing for two years. The younger brother heard him out with a smile on his face. The two boys followed the river-bank from the shipyard to Squire Wang's new grain mill. The elder brother said:

"No. 2, you're lucky to be Militia Captain Wang's prospective son-in-law and have this mill; as for me, if I do things right, I'll be inheriting from that old man the right to row a ferryboat. But I'd like that. I'd like to buy up the two hills at Green Creek Hill and plant stands of bamboo around the boundaries, fencing us in at our own little fortress by the stream!"

No. 2 continued listening in silence. He hacked at grasses and shrubs by the roadside with his sickle. When they reached the mill, he stopped and told his brother:

"Elder Brother, would you believe me if I told you that this girl already has her heart set on another, and has for some time?"

"Not a chance."

"Elder Brother, do you think this mill was meant for me?"

"No."

They entered the millhouse.

No. 2 continued: "Now don't . . . Well, Elder Brother, let me ask you again, suppose I didn't want this mill, but that ferryboat instead, and suppose, too, that I'd got this idea two years ago—would you believe that?"

Startled, the elder brother stared at his younger brother, Nuosong, sitting there on the horizontal axle of the mill roller. Realizing that No. 2 was telling him what was in his heart, he came up to him and clapped him on the shoulder, as if to bring him down to the ground. He understood now, and laughed. He said: "Now I believe you. Everything you've said is true!"

No. 2 looked back at his brother and said, with utter frankness:

"Elder Brother, believe me, this is the truth. This has been my plan for some time now. If her family agrees, even if ours doesn't, I truly mean to be a ferryman! What about you, then?"

"Papa has already acted on my behalf. He had Horseman Yang come from town to be my matchmaker and deliver my proposal to the ferryman!" When No. 1 got to the part about how he went about it, as if aware that No. 2 might laugh at him, he explained why he wanted a go-between to do it: "You see, the old man said that chariots must move like chariots and horsemen must move like horsemen. So I adopted the direct way, the chariot's move."

"What was the response?"

"There's none yet. The old man talked out of both sides of his mouth."

"What about adopting the horseman's move?"

"The old man said that the horseman's move means singing for the girl from the bluffs across the creek for three years and six months. If I could bend Cuicui's heart toward me, she'd be mine."

"What a good idea!"

"Maybe. Sometimes a stutterer can sing what he can't say. But that's not me. I'm no song sparrow; I haven't got the voice. Who the hell knows whether the old man would rather marry his granddaughter to a singing waterwheel or to a real man!"

"What are you going to do, then?"

"I'd like to see the old man and get a straight answer out of him. Just get the word. If 'No,' I'll take a boat downstream to Taoyuan. If 'Yes,' I'll agree, even if it means tugging that ferryboat."

"Would you sing for her?"

"Younger Brother, that's your strong suit. If you want to be a song sparrow, hurry up and get to it. I won't stuff your mouth with horse manure."

No. 2 could tell how upset his elder brother was. He knew his temper, which embodied the rough, straightforward side of the Chadong folk. In the right circumstances, he'd tear out his heart for you; cross him, and he'd battle his own maternal uncle blow for blow. If No. 1 met with failure after making the chariot's move, surely he would want to try the horseman's. But once he'd heard his younger brother's frank profession, he realized that No. 2 would best him at the latter approach. No. 1 hadn't a chance. Hence he was a little offended, a little indignant, and he couldn't hide it.

No. 2 had an idea: let the brothers go together to sing at Green Creek Hill one moonlit night, without letting on that there were two of them. They would sing in turn and whoever got a song in response could let his victorious lips take up the refrain for the ferryman's granddaughter. Since No. 1 was not much of a singer, when it was his turn, No. 2 would sing for him. What could be fairer than to let fate decide their future happiness? When he heard this proposal, No. 1, thinking that he could not sing for himself, didn't want his younger brother to be the song sparrow in his place. But No. 2, being of a poetic disposition, stubbornly insisted on this solution. He said this was the only way, for it was completely fair and impartial.

No. 1 thought about his younger brother's suggestion some more and smiled wryly. "Damn it all! I'm no song-bird—so I'm going to ask my little brother to be one for me?

All right, let's do it this way: we'll take turns singing, but I don't want any help from you. I'll do all my own singing. An owl in the forest can only screech, but when he wants a wife, he sings for himself, he doesn't hire a stand-in!"

Once in agreement, they picked the date. The moon would be fullest this night, the fourteenth, and the two nights following. It was midsummer; the nights were neither too hot nor too cool. Wearing plain white homespun undershirts, they'd ascend the high bluffs where the moon shined bright and, according to local custom, truthfully and earnestly sing for the girl—an unspoiled maiden, made unafraid by her innocence. When it was time for them to go home, as the dew fell and their voices grew weak, they would make their way back in the dimming moonlight. Or they might stop at a familiar grain mill that operated all night without rest, lying down to sleep in the cozy barn until daybreak. It was all so natural, and although neither brother could imagine the outcome, that would come just as naturally. They decided to do it that very night: engage in a competition honored by local custom.

CHAPTER THIRTEEN

Cuicui sat beneath the white pagoda behind her house as dusk fell, watching wispy clouds in the sky burned peach-blossom pink by the setting sun. The fourteenth of the month was market day at Middle Stockade. Many merchants from town went to that village fair to buy native products from the mountains, so ferry passengers were particularly abundant. Grandpa worked on the ferryboat without rest. As nightfall descended, the songbirds fell quiet: only the cuckoos sang on without cease. The mud on the boulder had dried in the sun the day long, and so had the trees and grasses. Now they were giving back their heat. The air smelled of damp soil, of the grasses and the trees, and also of beetles. Watching the pink clouds in the sky and listening to the jumble of voices from the merchants touring the countryside, Cuicui felt faintly despondent.

The dusk was as serene as always, just as beautiful and peaceful. Yet anyone in this situation would feel faintly despondent. And so the days became a time of unhappiness. Cuicui felt that she was missing something. As she saw the days pass before her, she seemed to want to be caught up in a new kind of human relationship, yet it was beyond her. Life seemed too dull and ordinary. She could bear it no longer.

"I want to sail a boat down past Taoyuan, across Lake Dongting. Let Granddad search for me all over town with a lantern, beating a gong and calling out my name."

Letting her imagination run wild with this impossible development, she seemed purposely angry at Grandpa. She went on to imagine him searching for her everywhere to no avail, until finally he would lie down in his boat in defeat.

Someone would shout, "Ferry me across, uncle. What's wrong with you? You're not doing your job!" "What's wrong? Cuicui is gone, she's gone down to Taoyuan County!" "What are you going to do about that?" "You know what? I'm going to pack a knife and catch a boat downstream, so I can kill her!"

Cuicui became as frightened as if she had really heard such a conversation. She shrilly called out for her grandpa, running from the ridge to the creek where the ferry landing was. When she saw Grandpa in midstream, tugging his ferryboat while the passengers talked softly on board, her little heart leaped up and down.

"Grandfather, pull the boat back to this side!"

The old ferryman didn't understand what was on her mind. Thinking she wanted to take over for him, he said,

"Cuicui, wait a little, I'll be back over!"

"Why aren't you coming back now?"

"I'm coming right away!"

Cuicui sat by the stream bank, observing everything out on the creek, which was now enveloped by the dusk. She also looked at the crowd of passengers on the ferryboat, including one who knocked the ashes out of his long-stemmed tobacco pipe by striking it against the side of the boat before lighting it with a sickle-shaped steel striker. She suddenly began to cry.

When Grandpa pulled the boat back to shore, he saw Cuicui sitting on the stream bank, staring into space. He asked what was the matter, but Cuicui didn't reply. Grandpa wanted her to light the fire and prepare supper. After thinking about it, Cuicui felt foolish for having wept. She went alone back into the house. She sat down in the pitch-black kitchen and lit the fire, then went back outside onto the high bluffs and called out for her grandpa to come home. But he did not come ashore. The old ferryman was too serious about his job for that. He knew that his passengers were all hurrying back to town for their meals. He ferried them as they came, one by one if necessary, so they wouldn't have to wait alone on the riverbank. Standing in the prow of the boat, he told Cuicui to stop yelling at him, to let him do his job. When he had got his passengers across, he would return home and eat supper.

Cuicui again begged Grandpa to come, but he paid no attention. She sat on the bluffs, feeling quite put out.

It was now completely dark. Blue light shone from the tail of a big firefly that flew past Cuicui in a burst of speed. She thought, "Let's see how far you can fly!" She followed the light with her eyes. Cuckoos began to sing again.

"Grandfather, why don't you come back? I want you here!"

When Grandpa heard her sweetly pleading voice, which bore a measure of reproach, he answered her gruffly: "I'm coming, Cuicui, I'm coming." Meanwhile he mumbled, under his breath, "Cuicui, when your grandfather is gone, what will you do then?"

When the old ferryman returned home, the kitchen was completely dark, lit only by flames from the stove. Cuicui was sitting there on a low stool, her face in her hands.

When he came closer, he realized that Cuicui had been crying for quite a while. Usually when Grandpa came home, stooped from pulling the boat all day long, with sore hands and an aching back, he'd smell vegetables stewing in the wok and see Cuicui dashing about in the lamplight, preparing supper. Today was a little different.

Grandpa continued, "Cuicui, I came in late, but is that any reason to cry? What if I were dead?"

Cuicui said nothing.

Grandpa went on: "No more crying! Act like an adult. No crying, no matter what. You have to be a little tougher, a little stronger, to get through life on this earth!"

Cuicui uncovered her eyes and cuddled up to Grandpa. "I've stopped crying."

While the two made supper, Grandpa told Cuicui some interesting stories. This led to talk of Cuicui's deceased mother.

After they'd finished their meal by the light of a soybean-oil lamp, the old ferryman, tired from his day of work, drank half a bowl of liquor. This picked up his spirits. He went outside with Cuicui and told her some more stories under the moonlight out on the bluffs. He told her about how lovely and good her poor mother had been, and also about her stubborn streak. Cuicui found it wholly absorbing.

Listening in the moonlight next to her grandpa, with her arms wrapped around her knees, Cuicui asked for more stories about her poor mother. Sometimes she would sigh, as if something heavy were weighing on her heart that she could move away with her breath. And yet she had no way to relieve her anxiety.

The moonlight was silvery and it shone everywhere. The bamboo stands in the mountains appeared black under the moon. From the thickets of grass came the chirping of insects, thick as rain. Occasionally, a warbler suddenly twittered from some hidden place, until the little bird seemed to realize that it was too late to be making noise and closed its eyes to go peacefully to sleep.

Feeling in good spirits this night, Grandpa kept telling

Cuicui his stories. He told of how the local people's songs, twenty years ago, were famous throughout the borderlands of Sichuan and Guizhou. Cuicui's father was the best singer of them all, able to summon up every kind of figure of speech to explain the travails of love and hate—he told her all about that, too. He also told her how her mother had loved to sing, how she and Cuicui's father had sung love songs to each other in broad daylight before they ever met, one while cutting bamboo on the mountain, the other while tugging the ferry-boat across the stream.

Cuicui asked: "Then what happened?"

Grandpa answered: "That would take a long time to tell. The important thing is that these songs gave us you."

After that, Grandpa fell silent. He did not add, "The songs gave us you, and then they took away your father and mother."

CHAPTER FOURTEEN

Exhausted by his work, the old ferryman slept. Cuicui, tired from crying, slept too. She could not forget the things Grandpa had spoken of. In her dreams, her soul drifted up on the strains of beautiful songs, seeming gently to float all about, up to the white pagoda, down to the vegetable garden, onto the boat—then it flew back, midway up the hanging bluffs—but for what purpose? To pick the "tigers' ears": saxifrage! While pulling the boat during the daylight hours, she looked up at those cliffs and became quite familiar with the huge saxifrage leaves there. The cliffs were thirty or fifty feet high, ordinarily too high to reach, but now she could pick the very biggest leaf and make an umbrella out of it.

Everything was happening just as in Grandpa's stories. Cuicui drifted off as she lay on a reed mat inside the burlap mosquito netting, taking pleasure in the beauty and sweetness of her dream. Grandpa, however, lay awake on his bed, straining his ears listening to late-night singing on the high cliffs across the stream. He knew who was singing: it was No. 1, Tianbao of River Street, making the horseman's move. He listened, both troubled and excited. Having worn herself out from crying during the day, Cuicui slept soundly, so Grandpa didn't disturb her.

Cuicui and Grandpa rose at dawn the next day and washed their faces in the creek to remove the taboo against telling one's dreams the morning after. Then Cuicui hastened to tell Grandpa what she had dreamed the night before.

"Grandfather, you told me stories about singing, and yesterday I heard the most beautiful songs in my dreams, soft and sweet. I felt I was able to fly in the air with these songs, to the face of the cliffs across the creek, where I picked a big saxifrage leaf. But once I picked it, I don't know who I gave it to. I slept wonderfully and dreamed magnificently!"

Grandpa smiled gently in sympathy, but did not tell Cuicui what had gone on the night before.

He thought to himself: "If only you could dream on forever. Some people become the prime minister in their dreams."

The old ferryman still thought it was Tianbao, No. 1, who had sung the night before. In recent days he had asked Cuicui to take charge of the ferry. Pretending to be delivering some medicines in town, he set off to find out what River Street was up to. There he ran into No. 1. He drew the young man aside, saying, cheerfully,

"No. 1, you dog, now you've tried both the chariot's move *and* the horseman's move. You're a sly one!"

But the old ferryman was wrong—he had confused one brother with the other. The night before, the two brothers had come to Green Creek Hill together. Because the elder brother had already made the first move, in the role of chariot, he insisted on letting his younger brother sing first this time. Realizing from the moment the latter raised his voice in song that he could never match him, No. 1 was more reluctant than ever to sing himself. The songs that Cuicui and her grandpa heard that night were all sung by No. 2, Nuosong. As No. 1 accompanied his younger brother home, he decided to leave Chadong and go downstream on the family's new oil boat, the better to forget what had happened. Just now, No. 1 was thinking of going to the docks to see cargo loaded onto the new boat. Noting his cold expression, the old ferryman, misunderstanding, gave an amused wink to let on that he knew that No. 1's cold-shouldering was pretend, and also to show that he had good news to impart. He clapped No. 1 on the back and whispered, sticking his thumb up,

"You sang so well that someone heard your songs in her dreams. The songs carried her far, far away, on many journeys! You're the best, the very best singer around!"

No. 1 stared back at the old boatman's unabashed expression and whispered:

"Enough. You can keep your precious granddaughter for some songbird."

The old ferryman had no idea what he meant by that. No. 1 went down a path between the stilt houses to the river, with the ferryman following. At the river, numerous bamboo oil casks were on the bank, waiting to be laded onto the new boat. A boatman was twisting strands of cogongrass into sheaves to make bulwarks that would keep waves from washing over the deck. Another man was sitting on a rock by the riverbank, greasing the oars with his hands. The old ferryman asked the boatman making the grass bundles when the boat would launch and who would pilot it. The boatman pointed to No. 1. The old ferryman rubbed his hands and said:

"No. 1, let me speak seriously, the chariot's move is not the right one for you. But you'll succeed with the horseman's move!"

No. 1 pointed his finger at a window above and said: "Uncle, look up there. If you want a songbird for your grandson-in-law, there he is!"

The old ferryman looked up and saw No. 2, who was mending a fishnet by the window.

When the ferryman reached the ferry at Green Creek Hill, Cuicui asked him:

"Grandfather, you've been quarrelling with someone. You look awful!"

Grandpa smiled, but said nothing about his trip to town.

CHAPTER FIFTEEN

No. 1 took the new oil boat downriver, leaving Nuo-song behind at home. The old ferryman thought that since No. 2 had sung the time before, he would sing again in the days to come. After nightfall he made a point of getting Cuicui to listen for songs in the night air. The two of them sat indoors after supper. Because their home fronted on the water, long-legged mosquitoes began buzzing at dusk. Cuicui lit bundles of wormwood incense and shook them in every corner of the house to drive away the insects. After shaking them until she thought the whole house was thoroughly smoked, she put some on the floor in front of her bed before sitting on a little wooden stool to listen to Grandpa tell his stories. The subject finally turned to singing, about which Grandpa was quite eloquent. Finally, he asked Cuicui, jokingly:

"Cuicui, the songs in your dream lifted you up the cliffs to pick saxifrage; if someone really sang to you from the cliffs across the stream, what would you do?"

Cuicui answered him in a similarly humorous vein: "I'd listen to him, for as long as he could sing!"

"What if he sang for three years and six months?"

"If his voice was good, I'd listen for three years and six months."

"That's not fair."

"Why not? Wouldn't he want me to listen to him for a long time?"

"They say that when you cook food, you want someone to eat it, and when you sing, you want someone to listen. But if a person sings to you, it's because he wants you to understand the meaning of the lyrics!"

"Grandfather, what meaning?"

"His true heart, of course, which wants your affection! If you don't grasp what's in his heart, would it be any better than listening to a songbird?"

"And what if I did happen to understand what's in his heart?"

Grandpa slapped his thigh and laughed: "Cuicui, you're a smart girl and your grandfather is plain stupid. If I speak a little too bluntly, don't get mad at me. I'll throw caution to the wind and tell you a funny story. No. 1, Tianbao of River Street, made the chariot's move; he had a go-between propose matrimony. When I told you about it, you didn't seem too willing, am I right? But if he had a younger brother who adopted the horseman's move and sang to you to win your heart, what would you say to that?"

Startled, Cuicui lowered her head. She didn't know how much of this story might be real, or who made it up.

Grandpa said: "See if you can come up with an answer—which one do you prefer?"

Forcing herself to smile, Cuicui replied softly, and somewhat pleadingly:

"Grandfather, no more of your humor." She stood up.

"Suppose it were not just a story but the truth?"

"Grandfather!" Cuicui walked away as she answered.

Grandpa said: "It was in jest! Are you angry at me?"

Cuicui could hardly be angry at him. When she got to the door, she turned the conversation toward something else: "Look how big the moon is, Grandfather!" She went outside and stood still in the bright and open air. After a time, Grandpa came outside to join her. Cuicui sat down on the great boulder—warmed by the hot sun during the day, it was radiating its spare heat now. Grandpa said,

"Cuicui, don't sit on the hot boulder or you'll get blisters."

But after feeling the rock, he sat down on the crag, too.

The moonlight was very gentle and a thin white mist floated on top of the stream. It would have been the perfect time for someone to sing from across the creek, and to be answered from the other side. Cuicui thought about the funny story her grandpa had told her. She was not deaf, and Grandpa had made his meaning quite clear. What did it mean if one of the brothers made the horseman's move and spent a night like this singing to her? She remained silent for a long time, as if waiting to hear such songs.

She sat there under the moonlight; she really wanted to be sung to. In the end, no sound came from the opposite bank other than the light drone of field insects. Cuicui went into the house and groped in the darkness for the *luguan* reed pipe. She brought it back out into the moonlight and began blowing on it. Feeling that her playing was not very good, she passed it to Grandpa. The old ferryman put it to his lips and played a long tune that softened Cuicui's heart.

She sat beside her grandpa and asked:

"Grandfather, who invented this little musical instrument?"

"It must have been the happiest person on earth, because happiness is what it gives; yet perhaps the world's unhappiest person, too, because it also makes people unhappy!"

"Grandfather, are you unhappy? Are you angry at me?"

"Not at all. Having you by my side makes me very happy."

"What if I ran away?"

"You wouldn't leave your grandfather."

"But just suppose I did. What would you do?"

"In the remote event that you did, I'd go looking for you in this ferryboat."

That brought a chortle from Cuicui.

*Phoenix Rapids, Puncture Vine Rapids, aren't the
     worst to rage,
Just go downstream and there is still the Twirling
     Chicken Cage;
But Twirling Chicken Cage yet lacks the most
     ferocious foam,
The waves at Green Foam Rapids are big as any
     home.*

"Grandfather, could your ferryboat make it through all those rapids on the River Yuan? Didn't you say that the river in those places is like a madman, simply unwilling to listen to reason?"

Grandpa said, "Cuicui, by the time I got there I'd be a madman myself. What would I have to fear from broad rivers and giant waves?"

Cuicui thought it over a little, seemingly in earnest, then said: "Grandfather, I wouldn't leave. But would you? Might someone carry you off?"

Grandpa didn't answer. He felt that he had nothing to fear from the law and the officials. Death was the one thing that might take him.

The old ferryman got to thinking about what would happen when death carried him away. Staring blankly at a star in the southern sky, he thought: "Shooting stars come only in the seventh and eighth months of the year. Might my death come then, too?" He also thought about his conversation with No. 1 on River Street that day, about the mill that was to be the dowry of the girl from Middle Stockade, and about No. 2—about a lot of things. He felt a little uneasy at heart.

Suddenly, Cuicui asked: "Grandfather, won't you sing a song for me, please?"

Grandpa sang ten songs. Cuicui listened by his side, her eyes closed. When he finished, she said to herself: "I've picked saxifrage again."

The songs Grandpa sang for her were the very songs they heard the night of her dream.

CHAPTER SIXTEEN

No. 2 now had his chance to serenade, but he never came to Green Creek Hill to sing again. The fifteenth passed, the sixteenth, then the seventeenth. Unable to bear the wait any longer, the old ferryman went to town and looked for the young fellow on River Street. When he got to the gate in the city wall and was about to enter River Street, he met Horseman Yang, who had been No. 1's matchmaker. He was heading out of town, leading a mule, when he saw the old ferryman and took him aside:

"Uncle, here you are come to town, just when I had something to discuss with you!"

"What?"

"That boat Tianbao took downstream was wrecked in the Puncture Vine Rapids. He fell into a whirlpool and drowned. Shunshun's family got the news this morning. I hear that No. 2 set off for the place at once."

This bad news stung the old ferryman like a heavy slap in

the face. He couldn't believe it. Feigning calm, he said,

"No. 1, drowned? Since when does a duck drown in water?"

"But that's just what happened to this duck . . . I salute your wisdom in not letting that young fellow have your granddaughter so easily, by the chariot's move."

The horse-soldier's words were not enough to still the old ferryman's doubts about the news, but he could clearly see from his expression that this was completely real. He said, grimly,

"What wisdom? This is the doing of Heaven! Everything is according to Heaven's will . . ." As he spoke, the old ferryman choked up.

To confirm the reliability of the horse-soldier's news, the old ferryman took leave of him and hurried over to River Street. People were burning paper spirit money in front of Shunshun's house. A crowd had gathered. Pressing in among them, the ferryman heard them talking about the tragedy of which Horseman Yang had spoken. Yet, as soon as they discovered that the old ferryman was listening in, they all changed the subject, unnaturally, to the price of oil in downstream markets. Nervous and worried, the old ferryman looked around for a boatman with whom he could talk on friendlier terms.

A short while later, Fleetmaster Shunshun arrived home, wholly dejected. This honest middle-aged man, ordinarily bold and gregarious, seemed beaten down by his misfortune. Struggling to go forward, he said, as soon as he saw the old ferryman:

"Elder Uncle, that plan of ours has fallen through. Tian-bao has met his end. Have you heard?"

His eyes red, the old ferryman wrung his hands: "What, so it's true? It can't be! Did it happen yesterday or the day before?"

Another man broke in, who appeared to be just back with the news: "The morning of the sixteenth, the boat got stuck on a reef and water came pouring over the bow. No. 1 was flipped into the water while trying to pole the boat free."

The old ferryman asked: "Did you see him fall into the water?"

"I fell in with him!"

"What did he say?"

"He had no time to speak! During the whole trip, he didn't say a word!"

The old ferryman shook his head and timidly looked at Shunshun. As if aware of his unease, Fleetmaster Shunshun said, "Uncle, it's all Heaven's doing. That's all there is to it. Someone from Daxingchang has given me a gift of fine wine. Take some home with you." One of the lads brought a bamboo tube full of wine and covered it with a fresh tung-tree leaf. He gave it to the old ferryman.

Taking the wine, the old ferryman went out onto River

Street, then bowed his head and walked toward the wharves
to find the place where Tianbao had boarded his boat three
days before. Horseman Yang was already there, keeping
cool in the shade of a willow tree while letting his horse roll
around on the sandy shore. The old ferryman walked over
and asked him to taste the wine from Daxingchang. After a
few swallows, when they were in better spirits, the ferryman
told Horseman Yang how on the night of the fourteenth the
two brothers had come to Green Creek Hill to sing.

When Horseman Yang heard this, he said,

"Uncle, don't you think Cuicui ought to go to No. 2,
since she's willing . . ."

He hadn't even finished his sentence when Nuosong, No.
2 himself, came down to the river. The young man looked as
if he were about to go on a long trip. Catching sight of the old
ferryman, he averted his gaze and went the other way. Horseman Yang called out to him, "No. 2, No. 2, over here, I'd like
to talk to you!"

No. 2 halted. Irritated, he asked the horseman, "What is
it?" The horseman looked at the old ferryman, then said to
No. 2, "Come here, I've got something to say!"

"What?"

"I'd heard you'd already gone—come over here so we can
talk, I won't bite you! When are you leaving?"

Nuosong, dark-faced, broad-shouldered, and full of life
and energy, forced a smile and came over under the willow.

Wanting to clear the air, the old ferryman pointed toward the new mill far upriver and said, "No. 2, I hear that mill will be yours in the future! When it is, what say you let me run it for you?"

As if irritated by what the old ferryman was driving at, No. 2 remained silent. Horseman Yang, seeing that they were headed toward an impasse, put in: "No. 2, how goes it, are you ready to set sail?" The young man nodded. He left without another word.

Realizing that he had brought about his own humiliation, the old ferryman returned to Green Creek Hill feeling very upset. When he reached the ferry, he pretended to have taken it all in stride as he told Cuicui:

"Cuicui, news has come from the city today. Tianbao, No. 1, took his oil boat downstream to Chenzhou and ran into some bad luck. He met his end in the Puncture Vine Rapids."

Not having understood his meaning, Cuicui at first seemed not to take Grandpa's report too seriously. So he added:

"It's true, Cuicui. Horseman Yang, who came here the time before as a matchmaker, even said that by not giving you away too soon, I showed a lot of foresight!"

A quick glance at Grandpa told Cuicui that his eyes were red. She knew he'd been drinking and also that something was troubling him. She thought, "Who got you so angry?" When the ferryboat reached the home side, Grandpa laughed unnaturally and went toward the house. Cuicui remained in the boat. Hearing nothing from Grandpa for a very long time, she headed home herself to have a look. She saw Grandpa sitting on the doorstep, plaiting straw sandals.

She could tell that Grandpa was not himself. She knelt in front of him.

"Grandfather, what's bothering you?"

"Tianbao is dead, don't you see. No. 2 is angry at us. He thinks we caused all this."

Someone at the stream hailed the ferry, so Grandpa hurried on out. Cuicui sat on a pile of rice straw in the corner of the house, greatly upset. When Grandpa didn't return, she began to cry.

CHAPTER SEVENTEEN

Grandpa seemed angry at someone. He didn't smile as much as before, and he didn't pay much attention to Cuicui. She began to realize that Grandpa was not doting on her as usual, yet she seemed not to understand the real reason for it. But this didn't last very long. Things got better as the days passed. The pair still spent their days on the ferryboat just as always, except that there seemed to be some invisible absence in their lives that simply could not be filled. When Grandpa went to River Street, Fleetmaster Shunshun still entertained him as before, yet it was quite apparent that the fleetmaster could never forget why his deceased son had come to be deceased. No. 2 had ventured two hundred miles down the White River to Chenzhou, searching for the corpse of his elder brother all along the way. It was in vain. After posting notices at all the customs stations, he returned to Chadong. Not long after, on his way to transport goods to East Sichuan, he came upon the old ferryman at the crossing. Observing that the young man seemed to have forgotten what had gone before, the old ferryman said to him,

"No. 2, traveling in the heat of the sixth month is terribly punishing, yet here you are on your way to East Sichuan again. I guess you can stand any hardship!"

"We have to eat. I'd have to be on my way even if the heavens above were on fire!"

"Eat? Don't tell me that's a problem in No. 2's family!"

"Oh, we have what we need, but Father says that young men ought not to stay home and eat without earning their keep!"

"How is your father these days?"

"He eats and works, as before. Why do you ask?"

"Ever since your elder brother's misfortune, the tragedy seems to me to have dealt your father a heavy blow!"

No. 2 was silent. He gazed at the white pagoda behind the old ferryman's house, as if recalling, wholly disconsolate, that night from the time before and the events that went with it.

The old ferryman stole a fearful glance at the young man and broke out in a smile.

"No. 2, my Cuicui tells me that one night during the last month she had a dream . . ." Watching No. 2 as he spoke, he saw neither shock nor irritation, so he went on: "It was strange. She said that in her dream someone's songs floated her up to the bluffs across the creek, where she picked a handful of saxifrage!"

No. 2 tilted his head and made a wry smile, thinking to himself, "This old codger is up to something." His suspicion was revealed in his smile and noted by the old ferryman, who continued, evidently flustered, "No. 2, don't you believe me?"

The young man replied: "Why wouldn't I believe you? I was a fool to sing all night long from the top of those cliffs!"

Shocked and humiliated by this unexpected bluntness, the ferryman stammered: "Really? . . . Surely not . . ."

"Oh no? What about the death of Tianbao? Isn't that real?"

"But, but . . ."

The old ferryman's pretenses had originally been aimed only at clarifying the situation a little, but from the start he sensed that he had done the wrong thing and been misunderstood. He wanted now to give a complete explanation of the events of that night, but the boat had reached the other bank. No. 2 wanted to be on his way as soon as he jumped to shore. The old ferryman shouted to him from the boat, all the more flustered:

"No. 2, No. 2, wait up, I have something to tell you. You know that part about you being a fool? You were no fool—it was your counterpart who went into a foolish rapture because of your songs!"

The young man paused a moment, but he said, softly: "That's it. Enough of this. Don't talk about it anymore."

The old ferryman continued, "No. 2, I heard that you'd rather tend a ferryboat than a grain mill. Horseman Yang told me so. Was he right?"

The young man said, "And what if I did want the ferry-boat?"

Suddenly cheered by the look on No. 2's face, the old ferryman couldn't resist loudly shouting for Cuicui to come down to the stream. But luck was not with him. He waited a long while and still there was no sign of her, and no response. She had either gone off or was purposely staying inside the house. No. 2 waited for a while in silence, watching the expression on the old ferryman's face, before smiling and striding off with a porter who was bearing loads of bean starch noodles and refined sugar.

Once they passed the low mountain called Green Creek Hill, the two took a winding path that skirted a bamboo grove. The porter spoke what was on his mind:

"Nuosong, I can tell from his look that this ferryman has really taken a liking to you!"

When No. 2 didn't answer, the man said:

"No. 2, he asked if you preferred the mill or the ferry. Are you really going to marry his granddaughter and take over his beat-up ferryboat?"

No. 2 laughed. The other man went on:

"No. 2, if it were my choice, I'd take the grain mill. There's a future in that. It'll make you three pints of rice and ten times that in bran."

No. 2 responded: "When I get back, I'll put in a word for you with my father. He can make you a match with those people in Middle Stockade, so you can have your mill. As for me, I'd be fine with that ferryboat. But the old man is too cunning by far. He's the one who led No. 1 to his demise."

The old ferryman was disconsolate to see No. 2 go on his way. Still Cuicui had not come out. He went to the house for a look and Cuicui was not there. A while later, Cuicui emerged from behind a hill, carrying a basket. He realized that Cuicui had been out all morning, digging up bamboo shoots.

"Cuicui, I called for you for the longest time! You must not have heard."

"What did you call me for?"

"There was a passenger on the ferry—someone we know. We got to talking about you. I called you, but you didn't answer!"

"Who was it?"

"Guess, Cuicui. He wasn't a stranger, you know him!"

Cuicui thought of the conversation she had inadvertently heard while in the bamboo grove just before. She blushed and for a long time remained quiet.

The old ferryman asked, "Cuicui, how many bamboo shoots did you gather?"

Cuicui turned her bamboo basket upside down. Besides a dozen or so little bamboo shoots, there was a big clump of saxifrage.

The old ferryman shot her a glance. Her cheeks flushing scarlet, Cuicui hurried away.

CHAPTER EIGHTEEN

As another month passed quietly by, the heartaches of all concerned seemed cured by the long summer days. The weather grew so hot that everyone was preoccupied with their sweating and they ate their fermented glutinous rice in cold water. There was no place left in their lives for heartaches and worries. Every afternoon, Cuicui took a nap on the shady side of the pagoda. It was very cool on that elevated spot. The soothing songs of bamboo finches and other birds came from the bamboo stands of the mountains on either side. The birds were such a numerous flock that in her dreams the mountain birdsong lifted her up into the air and brought her the most fantastic dreams.

There was no sin in that. Poets could spin out books of poetry from a small incident. Sculptors could carve the living image of a person in a piece of stone, and painters could turn out one magical painting after another from streaks of green, red, and gray. Who among them was not inspired by the memory of a smile, or a frown? Cuicui could not use writing, or stone, or colors, to transfer her heart's passions of love and hate into a work of art, she could only let her heart race ahead with the most absurd thoughts. This secretiveness often brought her an excitement both shocking and elating. A wholly unknowable future was shaking her emotions to their foundations, and she could not completely hide these passions from her grandpa.

As to Grandpa, one could say that he knew everything, but in fact he was wholly ignorant. He understood that Cuicui was not displeased with the No. 2 son, but he could not comprehend the young man's own disposition. He had met with rebuffs from both the fleetmaster and No. 2, yet he failed to be discouraged.

"If I can fix things up a little better, it will turn out all right, if only fate allows!" In that frame of mind, he mused that the course of love was never easy. The visions he dreamed with his eyes wide open were even more fantastic and unfettered than those of his granddaughter, Cuicui.

He inquired about the lives of No. 2 and his father from every local person who took his ferry, as solicitous about the River Street people as if they were family. Yet, strangely enough, this made him all the more fearful of actually running into them. When he did, he couldn't think of a thing to say. He rubbed his hands together nervously, as was his habit, having completely lost his composure. No. 2 and his father knew what he was up to, but the departed son, to use a cold expression, was chiseled into their hearts. They went about their business as the days passed by, acting as if they didn't know what the old ferryman was about.

Early in the morning, when it was obvious that he had not dreamed a single dream the night before, Grandpa would say,

"Cuicui, Cuicui, last night I had a simply awful dream."

"What awful dream?" Cuicui asked.

Then, pretending to be remembering his dream, he would scrutinize Cuicui's slender face and long eyebrows while telling her of a wonderful daydream he'd imagined at another time. Needless to say, none of these dreams were so fearsome after all.

All streams flow to the sea eventually. Although the conversation took a quite different direction to start, in the end it always came back to those matters that made Cuicui blush. Only when it became evident that Cuicui was displeased, her expression betraying embarrassment, did the old ferryman pretend that he was upset and hurry to explain himself, using small talk to cover up his intentions in bringing up these matters.

"Cuicui, that's not what I meant, not at all. Your grandfather is old and muddled, full of crazy talk."

But sometimes Cuicui quietly listened to Grandpa's crazy talk and muddled thoughts, to the point where she found herself smiling to herself.

She might suddenly blurt out:

"Grandfather, you really are mixed up!"

Hearing that, Grandpa would stop speaking. He meant to go on to say, "There are a lot of things on my mind," but before he could speak, he was summoned by a ferry passenger.

It was hot, so when ferry passengers from far away arrived bearing eighty-pound loads on their shoulder poles, they would rest and cool off by the creek. Squatting under the cliffs by the keg to enjoy a cool drink of tea, they passed their long "puffer" tobacco pipe between them while drawing the ferryman into their conversation. Thus did all sorts of baseless rumors, from the heavens above to the earth below, reach the old ferryman's ears. Sometimes the passengers would take advantage of the clean stream waters to wash their feet or bathe. The longer they stayed, the more gossip passed between them. Grandpa passed some of the talk on to Cuicui, and she learned a good deal in the process: the rise and fall of commodity prices, the going rate for riding a sedan chair or a boat, how to steer a timber raft down the rapids using its rudders, what it was like to look for a prostitute on an opium sampan, how ladies of the night with unbound feet boiled the opium—just about everything.

Nuosong, No. 2, returned to Chadong with his goods from East Sichuan. It was almost dusk and very still out on the stream. Grandpa and Cuicui were in the vegetable gar-

den, inspecting the turnip sprouts. Cuicui had napped a little
too long that day and was feeling a little forlorn, so when
she thought she heard a hoarse voice summon the ferry, she
was the first to go down to the landing. As she went down
the bank, she saw two men standing by the pier. She could
recognize them clearly in the light of the setting sun, though
their backs were to her: it was Nuosong, No. 2, and the family servant! Startled, like a little wild animal encountering a
hunter, Cuicui ran back into the bamboo grove on the hill.
But the two men at the stream turned around at the sound
of her footfall and saw everything. They waited a while and
still no one came, so the servant shouted again for the ferry
in his raspy voice.

The old ferryman heard him very clearly, but continued
squatting in the garden, counting his turnip sprouts. He found
it amusing. He'd seen Cuicui take flight and knew it must be
because she recognized someone at the landing. He purposely
kept on squatting under the high cliffs, ignoring the men.
Cuicui was young and not in charge; when she didn't respond
to the men who wanted to cross, they had no recourse but to
keep straining their voices to summon the ferry. After several more shouts, the hired man rested his tired voice and
asked No. 2, "What's this all about? You don't suppose the
old man is down sick and has left the ferry to Cuicui all by
herself?" No. 2 answered, "Let's wait, we're in no hurry!" So
they waited awhile. Because the passengers had fallen quiet,

the old ferryman in the garden thought to himself: "Could it be No. 2?" As if afraid of annoying Cuicui further, he kept on squatting there and didn't make a move.

But not long after, the shouting for the ferry resumed, and this time it sounded a little different. It was No. 2's voice. Was he angry? Tired of waiting? Had there been an argument? Frantically trying to size up the situation, the old ferryman raced down to the stream bank. When he got there, he saw the two men already aboard the boat, and one of them was No. 2. The old ferryman shouted out, anxiously,

"Hey there, No. 2, you're back!"

Showing his displeasure, the young man answered, "Yes, I'm back. What's wrong with you folks at the ferry? We waited forever and no one came for us!"

"I thought it was—" he looked all around and there was no trace of Cuicui, but just then the yellow dog ran out of the bamboo grove on the mountain, so he knew she had gone up there. He changed his drift and said: "I thought you had already crossed over."

"Already crossed over? Who would dare launch the boat without you?" said the servant. As he spoke, a waterfowl skimmed over the water. "That jade-green bird is headed toward its nest. We have to hurry back home in time for supper!"

"You're in time, you've got plenty of time to get to River Street." The old ferryman had already jumped into the boat. "Don't you want to inherit this ferryboat for your own?"

he thought, as he pulled on the cable and the boat left the shore.

"No. 2, it must have been a tiring trip!"

As the old ferryman spoke, No. 2 listened without letting on how he was feeling. When they reached the shore, the young man and his servant shouldered their loads and crossed over the hill without saying a word. The old ferryman took note of their coolness. He shook his fist at them behind their backs, shook it three times. He cursed them under his breath and pulled the boat back to his side.

CHAPTER NINETEEN

Cuicui's flight into the bamboo grove and the old ferryman's long delay in coming down to the landing suggested to Nuosong that his prospects here were not good. Although the old ferryman was constantly intimating that Nuosong "had a chance for success in this," the old man's hesitant explanations were very inept; they made No. 2 think of his elder brother, and he misinterpreted them. He felt a little aggrieved and a little angry. On his third day back home, someone arrived from Middle Stockade to sound him out. During an overnight stay in Shunshun's house on River Street, the man asked Shunshun where No. 2 stood—did he still want the new mill or not? Shunshun referred the question to No. 2 himself.

No. 2 answered, "Papa, if this is for you—if adding a mill and a woman to the household would make you happy, then you give the go-ahead. If this is for me, then I need to think it over and wait a few days before answering. I still don't know if I ought to take the mill or the ferryboat; perhaps my fate will only allow me to operate the boat!"

The man who'd come to sound them out marked these words and set out for Middle Stockade to report on his mission. When he came to the ferry at Green Creek Hill and saw the old ferryman, he recalled No. 2's words and couldn't help smiling to himself. On learning that the man was from Middle Stockade, the ferryman asked him what business he had in town.

The Middle Stockade man knew enough to be circumspect in his words:

"Nothing much, I just went to Fleetmaster Shunshun's house on River Street and sat a spell."

"They say one doesn't go to the Temple of the Three Buddhist Treasures without a good reason. If you sat down there you must have had something to say!"

"We did exchange some pleasantries."

"What did you talk about?" The other man said nothing further, so the old ferryman went on: "I hear that someone from Middle Stockade wants to give away a mill by the riverside, together with his daughter, to Shunshun down on River Street. Has there been any progress in that matter?"

The man from Middle Stockade grinned. "It's a done deal. I asked Shunshun. He's quite willing to join families with the man from Middle Stockade. Then he asked the young man . . ."

"And how did he feel about it?"

"He said: 'A mill and a ferryboat lie before me. Originally I wanted the ferry, but now I've decided on the mill. A boat is always on the move, whereas a mill stays in place.' That fellow has a head on him."

This man from Middle Stockade was a rice broker, good at weighing his words. He well knew what the "ferryboat" referred to, but he didn't let on. When he saw the old ferryman start to speak, the Middle Stockade man broke in first:

"Everything depends on fate. Human actions hardly have a hand in it. It's too bad that Shunshun's No. 1—such a handsome lad—had to drown in the river!"

This stabbed the old ferryman right in the heart. He swallowed the words he was about to speak. After the man from Middle Stockade had come ashore and gone on his way, the old ferryman stood dejectedly in the prow of his boat, dazed. Ruminating about how distant No. 2 had been the time before, he felt very upset.

Cuicui was quite happily occupied under the pagoda. She went up to the high bluffs, wanting Grandpa to sing to her from below, but he paid her no attention. She went down to the stream, sulking, until she saw that Grandpa for some unknown reason looked very dispirited. When Cuicui approached and Grandpa saw her dusky, happy face, he put on a semblance of a smile. But there was someone transporting goods awaiting the ferry on the other side, so Grandpa said nothing. He pulled the boat south across the stream in silence, until midway he broke out loudly into song. After ferrying the passenger, Grandpa jumped up on the dock and went up to Cuicui with a wry smile on his face again. He wiped his forehead with his hand.

Cuicui said,

"What's the matter, Grandfather, are you suffering from heatstroke? Lie down and rest in the shade! I'll take care of the boat."

"Yes, you take care of it. Fine. Excellent, this boat is yours to take care of!"

He felt like he really did have heatstroke. He was sick at heart. Though he put up a strong front before Cuicui, when he was alone in the house he found a piece of broken porcelain, cut himself in a few places on his arms and legs to let out some blood, then lay down to sleep.

Taking up her post on the boat, Cuicui felt strangely euphoric. She thought: "If Grandfather won't sing for me, I'll sing myself."

She sang a good many songs. Lying in bed with his eyes shut and listening closely, the old ferryman grew anxious. But he knew that this illness would not be the end of him; he would still be able to get up tomorrow. He decided to go to town the next day and look around on River Street. He also mulled over many other matters.

When the morning came, however, though he left the

bed, his head still hung heavy. Grandpa was truly ill. Cuicui, knowing just what to do, boiled up a pot of fever-breaking herbal medicine and made Grandpa drink it. She also went out back to the garden to pick sour garlic sprouts for steeping in rice broth, as a cure. She frequently took time out from minding the boat to return home and look in on Grandpa and ply him with questions. But he had nothing to say; a secret pained him. Yet, after three days in bed, he was well. He seemed strong as ever as he paced in front and back of the house, but something was worrying him, so he prepared to journey to River Street. Cuicui couldn't understand what could be so important as to make Grandpa go to town so soon. She begged him not to go.

The old ferryman rubbed his hands together, wondering whether he ought to tell her what his business was. Standing before Cuicui, with her bright eyes and dark, oval face, he had to sigh.

"I have something important to do," he said, "and I have to go today!"

Cuicui smiled disdainfully: "What's so urgent? Surely it's not . . ."

The old ferryman knew his granddaughter's temper; he could hear the unhappiness in her voice, so he stopped insisting on going. Laying on the table the bamboo tube and embroidered cloth shoulder bag he'd prepared for the trip, he said, with a fawning smile, "All right, I won't go. Since you're afraid I might fall down dead, I won't go. I thought I'd go to town in the morning, before it got too hot, and finish my business—but I don't have to go. I can go tomorrow!"

Cuicui replied, softly and gently, "Yes, tomorrow will be fine. Your legs are still weak! A day's rest will do you good."

Seeming not really willing to give in, the old ferryman shrugged and stepped away. As he crossed over the high door threshold, he nearly tripped headlong over the stick he used to make straw sandals. When he'd steadied himself, Cuicui put on a pained smile and said: "Grandfather, you see, you still don't know how to take advice!" The old man picked up the stick and threw it into a corner of the room, adding: "Your grandfather may be old, but just wait a few days, and I'll hunt you a leopard!"

In the afternoon it rained, but the old ferryman said good-bye to Cuicui and went to town anyway. Since Cuicui couldn't go with him, she insisted that the yellow dog accompany him. Once in town, he was detained by a friend who wanted to talk about the price of salt and rice. Then he went to the army barracks to see the new mules and horses purchased by the head of the *likin* tax bureau before he finally got to Shunshun's house on River Street. There he found Shunshun playing cards with three other men. Unable to speak to him in private, he just stood behind Shunshun and looked at his hand. After a while Shunshun invited him for a drink, but the ferryman begged off, on the excuse that he had been sick. The card players weren't ready to go home and the old ferryman wasn't about to leave, either. Shunshun seemed unable to figure out why he had come; he just concentrated on his hand. It was another man who took note of the old ferryman's discomfort and asked if he had something to discuss. That made the old ferryman rub his two hands together nervously, as was his habit, and say, not really, he just wanted to exchange a word or two with the fleetmaster.

The fleetmaster finally understood why the ferryman had been standing behind him, looking at his cards for so long. He turned around and smiled at the old ferryman.

"Why didn't you say so? You didn't say anything, so I thought you must be trying to learn a few tricks of the game."

"It's nothing, just a little something I wanted to talk about. I didn't want to spoil the fun—didn't dare interrupt you."

The fleetmaster threw his cards down on the table. Smiling, he went into the back room, with the old ferryman following behind.

"What's on your mind?" the fleetmaster asked, with an expression hinting that he knew what the boatman was about to say, and also bearing a touch of pity.

"I heard a man from Middle Stockade say you were preparing to link your family in marriage with the militia captain there. Is it true?"

The fleetmaster could see the old ferryman's eyes fixed on

him, begging for the answer he wanted. "You've heard right," said the fleetmaster. But the implication was, "What's it to you?"

"That's a fact?" the old ferryman asked.

"True enough," the other said, unconcernedly. But the implication, again, was another question: "Fact is, what business *is* it of yours?"

Pretending to be completely unruffled, the old ferryman asked, "What does No. 2 say?"

The fleetmaster replied: "No. 2 has taken a boat down to Taoyuan and been gone for several days now!"

As it happened, No. 2 had gone downriver to Taoyuan only after quarreling with his father. The fleetmaster might be extremely open-minded, but that didn't mean he was willing to have the girl who had killed his first son, even if indirectly, become the wife of his second; that was very clear. Local custom held that these things were all up to the younger generation—the elders were not to interfere. No. 2 was truly fond of Cuicui, and Cuicui loved No. 2 also. The fleetmaster was not opposed to this sort of love match. But for some reason, the old ferryman's concentration on the matter had made both father and son misunderstand his motives. Whenever the fleetmaster thought of his recent family tragedy, he associated it with this old and meddlesome boatman. There was no outward sign of it, but inwardly there was a big hitch.

Without letting the old ferryman continue, the fleetmaster told him, somewhat bluntly:

"Uncle, no more of this. Our mouths are for drinking, not singing the young folks' songs for them! I know exactly what you mean to say, and you mean well. But I'm asking you to understand my position. We should talk about matters that are up to us, not try to pull strings for our youngsters."

After this final blow, the old ferryman still had something to say, but the fleetmaster wouldn't let him speak another word; he pulled him back to the card table.

The old ferryman was speechless. He looked at the fleetmaster, who was smiling and telling lots of jokes, but the way he threw down his cards showed his distress. Without another word, the old ferryman donned his conical hat and left.

It was still early, so the dejected old man went back into town to find Horseman Yang. He was drinking. The old ferryman pleaded that he was still sick, but couldn't help drinking a few cups of liquor anyway. Feeling hot from the walking by the time he got to Green Creek Hill, he washed himself in the stream. He was tired, so he asked Cuicui to keep on tending the boat while he went home and slept.

As dusk fell, the weather became quite oppressive. The stream was covered with red dragonflies. Mist was already gathering and hot winds were noisily rustling the bamboos in the mountain groves on either side of the stream. It looked as if it would rain that night. Cuicui was with the boat, watching the dragonflies as they flitted across the creek. Her heart was ill at ease, too. Seeing Grandpa so dejected, she grew worried and hurried home. She thought he would already be in bed, but he was sitting on the doorstep, weaving straw sandals!

"Grandfather, how many shoes do you need? Aren't there fourteen pairs up by your bed as it is? Why don't you lie down and rest?"

Instead of answering, the old ferryman stood up and looked at the sky. He said, softly: "Cuicui, there'll be a heavy thunderstorm tonight! Let's tie up our boat under the cliffs. The rain tonight is going to be heavy."

Cuicui said, "Grandfather, I'm afraid!" But what Cuicui feared didn't seem to be the coming thunderstorm.

Acting as if he hadn't understood her, the old ferryman said, "What's there to be afraid of? What will be will be. Don't be scared."

CHAPTER TWENTY

The night did bring a great storm, accompanied by frightening thunderclaps. Lightning swept over the rooftop, followed by a deafening crash of thunder. Cuicui quivered in the dark. Grandpa woke up, too. Sensing her fear, and worried that she might catch cold, he got up to cover her with a sheet. Grandpa said:

"Cuicui, don't be afraid!"

Cuicui replied, "I'm not." Meanwhile she thought to herself: "Grandfather, I'm not afraid because you're here!"

There came another roll of thunder, and then, overpowering the sound of the rain, the deadening sound of something giving way. Both of them were sure that the hanging cliffs by the stream bank must have caved in! They feared that their boat was crushed under collapsing rocks from the cliffs.

Grandfather and granddaughter kept silent in their beds, listening to the sound of the rain and thunder.

Even with the downpour, Cuicui was soon asleep again.

When she woke up, it was already daylight. The rain had stopped without her noticing. She heard only the sound of torrents from the gullies entering the stream from the mountains on both sides. Cuicui got up out of bed. Seeing Grandpa still sound asleep, she opened the door and went out. The ground in front of the house had become a ditch and water splashed past in a muddy stream from behind the pagoda, having come straight down from the bluffs. Newly formed channels of water were everywhere. The vegetable garden was flooded, its sprouts all covered with sand and gravel. Going over to the stream, she could see that the water had risen so high that it was already brimming over the dock. Soon it would reach the tea vat. The path down to the dock was like a little river, splashing yellow mud. The cable over the stream used to pull the boat across was already under water, and the ferryboat, previously tied up beneath the cliffs, was nowhere to be found.

Observing that the bluffs in front of the house had not collapsed, after all, Cuicui at first failed to notice that the ferryboat had disappeared. But as she looked up and down for it, she involuntarily turned around, and the white pagoda behind the house was gone. Startled by the enormity of the loss, she hurried out to the back of the house. The pagoda had collapsed into a big mass of bricks and stones. Cuicui was too scared to know what to do next, so she shrilly called out for her grandpa. When Grandpa did not get up or answer her, she ran into the house and shook him back and forth. Still he made no sound. The old man had died as the thunderstorm faded away.

Cuicui began to wail.

Before long, someone going on business from Chadong to East Sichuan arrived at the stream and called out for the ferry. Cuicui was at the stove, crying as she heated water with which to wash the corpse of her grandpa.

The man thought the ferryman's family must be asleep and he was in a hurry to cross. When his calls went unanswered, he threw a stone across the stream onto the roof of the house. Sniveling and crying, Cuicui ran out and faced the high cliffs by the stream.

"Hey, it's late! Bring the boat over!"

"The boat has left us!"

"Where's your grandfather? He's in charge of the boat. It's his responsibility!"

"Yes, it's his responsibility, and he did it for fifty years— and now he's dead!"

Cuicui blubbered as she spoke to the man on the other side of the stream. When he heard that the old ferryman had died, he realized he must return to town and report the news. He said:

"Is he really dead? Don't cry, I'll go back to town and tell people. They'll get you a boat and whatever else you need!"

When he got back to Chadong, he reported the news to every friend in sight, and soon everyone knew about it, inside the town and out. Fleetmaster Shunshun of River Street sent someone to find an empty boat. Carrying a plain, unpainted coffin, it was dispatched right away, to be poled upriver to Green Creek Hill. Horseman Yang and an old soldier hurried over to the site on their own, where they felled several dozen giant bamboos and bound them together with vines to form a raft as a temporary ferryboat. When the makeshift raft was ready, they poled it to the shore outside Cuicui's house. The old soldier manned the raft for ferry passengers, while Yang hurried to Cuicui's house to see the deceased. His eyes brimming over with tears, he stroked his dead friend, now stiff as a board, as he lay in bed. Then he busied himself making the necessary preparations. Others came to help out, and the coffin arrived on the boat sent over from the big river. An old Daoist priest from town ferried across on the raft, bringing his ritual musical instruments, an old sackcloth Daoist robe, and an old rooster, the better to intone scripture, make his waterside pronouncements, and fulfill his other ritual duties. People came and went from the house. Cuicui simply sat on a low stool by the hearth, sobbing.

Come noon, Fleetmaster Shunshun arrived, too, following a servant who carried a bag of rice, a vat of wine, and a large slab of pork hindquarters. He said to Cuicui:

"Cuicui, I heard about your grandfather's death. Death happens to us all when we get old. Don't you worry, I'll take care of you!"

He looked around and went home. In the afternoon, the body was put into the coffin. People who had come to help began returning home. By evening, the only ones left were the old Daoist priest, Horseman Yang, and two young workers that Shunshun had sent over from his house. Before dusk fell, the old priest cut out some flower shapes from red and green paper and fashioned candlesticks from yellow mud. When it was dark, a yellow candle was lit on the small table in front of the casket. There was incense, and other little candles were lit all around the coffin as the old Daoist priest put on his blue hempen gown and began the funeral rite of circling the coffin. The old priest went in front, carrying a paper streamer to lead the way, followed by the filially pious daughter and the horseman in the rear, slowly going in a circle around the lonely casket. The two hired men stood in an empty space by the stove, clanging a gong and cymbals to make noise. The old Daoist walked with his eyes closed, singing and chanting to comfort the spirit of the deceased. When he got to the part about the deceased spirit going to the Western Paradise, where fragrant flowers bloomed all year long, the old horseman raised high a wooden tray of the paper flowers and scattered them over the coffin, to symbolize the bliss of paradise.

At midnight, the ceremony came to an end. They set off firecrackers and the candles nearly burned out. With tears still streaming down her face, Cuicui hastened to the kitchen to stoke the fire and prepare a midnight meal for those who had assisted. After the meal, the old priest lay down in the bed of the deceased and slept. The others attended the coffin through the night, as was the custom. The old horseman sang funeral songs to help the others pass the time, tapping out the rhythm on a wooden grain measuring cup as his drum. He sang songs about children who were legendary exemplars of filial piety: about Wang Xiang, who lay naked on top of ice to catch a fish for his mean stepmother, and little Huang Xiang, who fanned the pillow of his sick father against the heat and warmed him with his own body to ward off the cold.

Completely exhausted from crying and working the live-long day, Cuicui rested her head on the front of the coffin and drifted off to sleep, but the two hired hands and the horseman, having eaten and drunk a few cups of wine, were in high spirits. They traded off singing their funeral songs. Cuicui suddenly reawakened, as if from a dream. She came to the terrible realization that Grandpa was dead, whereupon she took up her anguished weeping again.

"Don't cry, Cuicui, that won't bring him back!"

The old horseman went on to tell a joke about a bride crying on her wedding day, spiced up with a few vulgar expressions that had the two workers howling with laughter. The yellow dog barked outside the house. Cuicui went out and looked up. The air buzzed with the sound of insects. The moonlight was grand and bright stars were inlaid in the dark blue sky, creating an atmosphere of calm and serenity. Cuicui thought to herself:

"Can it be true? Is Grandfather really dead?"

The old horseman had followed her outside, for he knew that girls did not always show their emotions. A fire might linger under the embers without a trace; with her grandpa gone, and having lost all hope for herself, she might jump off the bluffs or hang herself, following Grandpa in death. How could they know? Therefore, he kept a constant watch over Cuicui.

Seeing Cuicui standing there in a daze and not turning to him for a long while, the old horseman coughed and said,

"Cuicui, the dew is falling. Aren't you cold?"

"I don't feel cold."

"It *is* fine out here!"

"Oh!" she exclaimed softly, seeing a big shooting star.

Then, in the south, another shooting star coursed down to earth. An owl hooted on the opposite shore.

"Cuicui," the old horseman said to her softly, having already come up beside her: "Go indoors and sleep a while. Don't let your thoughts run wild!"

Cuicui quietly returned to her grandpa's coffin. She sat on the floor and began sobbing again. The two workers standing guard in the house were already fast asleep.

The horseman said, faintly: "Don't cry! Don't! You'll break your grandfather's heart. It's no good to cry your eyes red and your voice hoarse. Listen, I know exactly what your grandfather intended. Leave it all to me. I'll arrange everything so it works out right, so I can face your grandfather. I'm up to it—I can do whatever is needed. I want this ferryboat to go to someone that your grandfather liked and that you like. If someone gets in the way, I may be old, but I can still wield my scythe and deal with him. Don't worry, Cuicui, I'll take care of everything!"

Somewhere far away, a cock crowed. The old Daoist priest mumbled to himself, half asleep, in bed: "Is it daylight? Time to rise and shine!"

CHAPTER TWENTY-ONE

Bright and early the next day, friends came from town, bringing ropes and carrying poles.

Fleetmaster Shunshun, the horseman, Cuicui, the old Daoist, and the yellow dog followed behind as six bearers carried the old ferryman's small, unvarnished coffin to the hill behind the collapsed pagoda for burial. When they got to a pit that had been dug to receive the body, the old Daoist priest jumped down into it and, according to custom, sprinkled flecks of cinnabar and white rice in the four corners and the center before burning a little spirit money. Then he crawled up out of the grave to let the bearers lower the coffin. Unable to summon up any more tears, Cuicui cried hoarsely and threw herself across it, refusing to get up. The coffin could be moved only after the horseman forcefully drew her aside. After that the coffin was lowered, with the ropes being tugged this way and that to square it in the pit. Fresh earth was piled on top as Cuicui remained sitting on the ground, sobbing.

The Daoist priest had to hurry back to town via the ferry to perform rites for sending another dead soul up to heaven. The busy fleetmaster, after entrusting the affairs on this side of the stream to the old horseman, likewise hurried back to town. All those who had been helping out went down to the stream to wash their hands. Each household had its own affairs to tend to, and they knew it was not the time for more polite words that would upset the next of kin, so they took the ferry home, too. That left behind only three people at Green Creek Hill: Cuicui, the old horseman, and Baldy Chen, also known as Fourth of the Fourth from his birth date, whom the fleetmaster had sent to temporarily tend the ferry. Having felt the sting of a stone cast by the bald man, the yellow dog, nursing his resentment, softly yelped to express his unhappiness.

Cuicui had a talk with the old horseman that afternoon. She pleaded with him to return to town and get someone else in camp to take care of his horses, so he could return to Green Creek Hill to stay with her. When the old horseman got back, Baldy Chen was dispatched back to town.

Cuicui and the yellow dog went back to operating the ferry, letting the old horseman amuse himself on the high bluffs or sing her songs in that old, gravelly voice of his.

Three days later, the fleetmaster came to propose that Cuicui come live in his house, but Cuicui, who wished to tend her grandpa's grave, wasn't ready to move. Instead she wanted the fleetmaster to speak to the government offices, to ask that Horseman Yang be allowed to live with her for the time being. Fleetmaster Shunshun agreed and went on his way.

Well past fifty now, Horseman Yang was an even better storyteller than Cuicui's grandpa. He was neat and diligent in his work and conscientious about everything; he made Cuicui feel that in losing a grandfather, she had gained an uncle. When the ferry passengers inquired about her poor grandpa, or when she got to thinking about him at nightfall, she felt miserable and dejected. But as the days passed, her misery weakened a little. As the horseman sat with the girl on the high bluffs by the stream every evening in the dusk and in the darkness, telling her stories about the poor old man lying in the wet soil, many of which she had never heard before, Cuicui's heart was put at ease. And he told Cuicui about her father, the soldier who valued both romantic love and honor, and how he had turned the local girls' heads in that smart uniform of his, the outfit of a brave in the Army of the Green Standard. He also told Cuicui about her mother—what a wonderful singer she was, and how the melodies and lyrics she made up were repeated far and wide.

But times had changed, and with them, all the local customs. If the emperor no longer ruled over the hills and valleys, how tumultuous had it been for ordinary folk! Horseman Yang recalled that when he was a young man and just a groom, he had led his horse to Green Creek Hill and sung to Cuicui's mother, but she paid him no attention. And now he was this young orphan's sole support and intimate. He couldn't suppress a knowing smile.

Because the two talked every evening at dusk, of Grandpa and everything about the family, and finally all that had happened before the old ferryman's death, Cuicui came to understand many things that Grandpa hadn't dared to mention while he was alive. No. 2's singing on the bluffs; the death of No. 1; the subsequent aloofness of Shunshun and his son toward Grandpa; the grain mill offered by the Middle Stockade captain as a dowry to entice Nuosong; how No. 2, remembering the death of his elder brother and feeling ignored by Cuicui, was pressed by his family to take the mill yet still preferred the ferryboat, until he fled downstream in anger; and how her grandpa's death had something to do with Cuicui . . . all that Cuicui hadn't been able to understand, now became clear. Once Cuicui understood, she cried the whole night long.

When the fourth week of mourning had passed, Fleetmaster Shunshun sent a man to ask the horseman back to town. He proposed that Cuicui come into his home, as the future wife of No. 2. But since No. 2 was in Chenzhou, they could not announce it; they would first have to ask No. 2 how he felt. The horseman thought that they should ask Cuicui first. When Horseman Yang got back and told Cuicui of Shunshun's proposal, he advised her not to move to a stranger's house while her fate was so unsettled; best to stay at Green Creek Hill until No. 2 sailed home, to hear his opinion.

That settled, and the old horseman thinking that No. 2 would soon return, he entrusted his horses to someone else at camp and stayed at Green Creek Hill to keep Cuicui company. The days passed.

The white pagoda at Green Creek Hill was important to the feng shui of Chadong. It was, of course, imperative that a new pagoda be built there. The military camp, the revenue bureau, and all the shops and ordinary citizens contributed money. All the big stockades brought in money, too. The pagoda was meant to confer blessings and advantages not just on particular people; everyone should be able to accumulate merit by contributing, so everyone was given the opportunity. Therefore a big bamboo tube with knots at each end and a slot sawed into its middle was put on board the ferryboat, to let passengers contribute money as they pleased. When the tube was full, the horseman brought it with him when he went to town to see his superiors—and carried a new one on his way back. Passengers, taking note that the ferryman was absent and that Cuicui had tied up her pigtails with white mourning ribbons, realized that the old man had completed his work in this life and was lying at peace in a mound of earth to feed the worms. They'd look sympathetically at Cuicui as they scrounged up a few coins for the bamboo tube. "May Heaven protect you. The deceased has gone to the Western Paradise.

Eternal peace to the living." Grasping the compassion and sympathy in their words, but sick at heart, Cuicui was quick to turn away and tug the boat.

Come winter, the white pagoda that had collapsed was good as new. The young man who had sung under the moonlight, softly lifting up Cuicui's soul from her dreams, had not yet returned to Chadong.

He may never come back; or perhaps he will be back tomorrow!

Notes to *Border Town*

This translation is based on the most critically acclaimed 1936 edition of Shen Congwen's 1933–34 novel, with a few corrections from his final revision in the 1983 edition of his collected works, which revised the characters' ages and so forth. The translator is grateful for help from Susan Corliss, Tim Duggan, Howard Goldblatt, Mi Hualing, and Shen Congwen's granddaughter Shen Hong.

p. x: [Border Town] *was banned in China ca. 1949–1979, and in Taiwan until 1986.* After political pressure induced him to attempt suicide in 1949, Shen Congwen prudently took up a new career in art history at the National Historical Museum in Beijing. Printing plates for his old literary works were destroyed, but his stories were not generally dangerous to possess until the Cultural Revolution, as they were at times in Taiwan, where the Nationalist government held that Shen was a Communist because he stayed on the mainland. Taiwan publishers challenged this censorship with at least one small printing of the relatively apolitical *Border Town*. A surprising recent

revelation from the mainland is that the Shanghai Cultural
Film Studio had a short-lived plan to film *Border Town* as
late as 1950, reviving a 1947 project with a new screenplay by
Shi Tuo. Radicalization of the revolution stopped that. The
first film version of *Border Town*, titled *Cuicui* (1953), came
from Hong Kong. For more about Shen Congwen in English,
see the translator's biography, *The Odyssey of Shen Congwen*;
A History of Modern Chinese Fiction, by C. T. Hsia; *Shen
Ts'ung-wen*, by Hua-ling Nieh; and *Fictional Realism in 20th
Century China*, by David Der-wei Wang. See the anthology
Imperfect Paradise for a selection of Shen Congwen's short
stories.

p. 1: *Chadong*. In real life, there is a town called Chadong ("Tea
Cave") at this location. Shen Congwen writes the name's second syllable with a similar but rarer and more picturesque
Chinese character containing the ideogram for "mountain"
and pronounced *tong* or *dong*. With the *dong* reading, the
town name likewise literally means "Tea Cave."

p. 4: *she had grown to be thirteen*. The Chinese says fourteen
sui. In the old way of counting, a person was one *sui* at birth
(acknowledging the time in-utero) and gained one more *sui*
("year old") every New Year. Hence ages in *sui* were a year or
more older than years elapsed since birth.

p. 10: *Chenzhou*. The city today called Yuanling.

p. 16: *"Dragon Head" lodge master*. A designation later attached
to the character Shunshun that likely indicates his status in
the Gelaohui, or Elder Brothers Society, a "secret society."
Later in the novel, he is addressed as Fleetmaster (*chuanzong*),
a term Shen Congwen explains as wharf-side argot for the actual, working boss of the river—an unofficial position. Shun-

shun is also described as Dockmaster, a more official role that Shen says was often a sinecure.

p. 18: *Forty-ninth army regiment.* A New Army regiment of Hunanese in the late Qing that joined the 1911 revolution to overthrow the monarchy. Following the revolution, most of China was beset by warlord depredations, large-scale banditry, and civil war.

p. 24: *wine mixed with realgar.* Realgar (arsenic sulfide), an ancient Chinese medicine thought to ward off evil, was sometimes taken internally, the wine diluting the poison. The approach of summer was associated with the spread of disease, from which children especially needed protection.

p. 25: *Liang Hongyu, Niu Gao, Yang Yao.* Several popular novels tell of the historical figure Liang Hongyu giving naval drum signals to help her husband, a Song dynasty general, trap enemy Jin forces as they fled up the Laoguan River. Histories also tell of Niu Gao, another Song dynasty general, under Yue Fei, who fought the Jin and captured the rebel Yang Yao in 1135 after he jumped into a river to commit suicide.

pp. 29, 57: *"Dragon Boat tide."* High waters said to arrive on the second or third day of the fifth lunar month.

p. 36: *"And your dog barked at him, having no idea who he was!"* Literally, "Your dog didn't know he was barking at Lü Dongbin," one of China's legendary Eight Immortals. The worker may have been thinking of another anecdote, about Lü Dongbin and a friend whose name was homophonous with "dog biting."

p. 42: *zongzi.* Dumplings made of sticky rice, often filled with meat, eggs, and vegetables, shaped like a pyramid and wrapped in palm leaves. They commemorate food that, according to legend, was thrown into the river in memory of Qu Yuan, the ancient virtuous and wronged minister who drowned himself in a river in Hunan and whose legend is honored on Duanwu, the fifth day of the fifth month, the Dragon Boat Festival.

p. 46: *Zhen'gan town.* The old, pre–1911 name for Fenghuang, Shen Congwen's beloved hometown.

p. 49: *Song Family Stockade.* "Stockade," *zhai*, is the local term for a village up in the Miao pale. These mountain settlements used to be fortified.

p. 55: *"She's a real Guan Yin."* Guan Yin was the goddess of mercy, a beauty in Buddhist iconography.

p. 64: *Lord Guan.* Guan Yu is a heroic general in the popular novel *Romance of the Three Kingdoms.* The same novel made famous the Red-haired Steed, which was the mount of General Lü Bu.

p. 64: *General Weichi Gong.* A Tang dynasty general who became one of China's two Door Gods. He brandishes an iron whip, but so does a famous character in *Romance of the Three Kingdoms,* Huang Gai.

p. 64: *Old Man Zhang Guo, Iron Crutch Li.* Immortals in the Daoist pantheon.

p. 65: *Hong Xiuquan, Li Hongzhang.* Taiping rebel Hong Xiuquan and Qing official Li Hongzhang are actual nineteenth-century historical figures. This mixing of "apples and oranges"—of sacred and profane, of history, myth, fiction, and misremembering—is presented in a tone of affectionate amusement regarding folk conceptions of history and culture.

p. 68: *Captain Zhang Heng.* A robber of boats in the popular novel *Water Margin* or *Outlaws of the Marsh*, who ended up a naval leader of the heroic band of outlaws in the novel.

p. 68: *Mount Liang.* The mountain redoubt of the 108 bandit heroes in *Water Margin.*

p. 71: *nanmu tree.* An evergreen strongly resistant to decay, used to make furniture and boats.

p. 79: *Lu Ban.* A fifth-century B.C.E. carpenter, philosopher, statesman, legendary inventor, and legendary builder of the Zhaozhou Bridge—but not, even in legend, the Luoyang Bridge, which was built after 1000 C.E.

p. 80: *for "three years and six months,"* i.e., "at length." Here the ferryman alludes to a West Hunanese mountain song Shen Congwen cited in his "Songs of the Zhen'gan Folk" (1926), translated in Jeffrey C. Kinkley, ed., *Imperfect Paradise* (Honolulu: University of Hawai'i Press, 1995), pp. 485–519.

> *You don't know as many songs as I do,*
> *I know as many as there are hairs on three oxen!*
> *If I sang for three years and six months,*
> *I'd just make it through three ears' worth!*

p. 84: *"people eat what they like, even beef with chives."* This local expression alludes to a folk belief that the combination is harmful to digestion, if not toxic.

p. 99: *Horseman Yang.* Mountainous West Hunan had no cavalry to speak of, but horses were ridden by commanders and used for transport. The Chinese word indicates that Yang's title was that of a full-fledged soldier.

p. 101: *he'd battle his own maternal uncle.* Relations with one's mother's brother(s) were particularly close in local society.

p. 102: *an unspoiled maiden, made unafraid by her innocence.* The Chinese phrase is "a newborn calf," which is said to be unafraid of anything, even tigers.

p. 107: *warbler.* Technically, a rufous-rumped grassbird.

p. 108: *After that, Grandpa fell silent. He did not add, "The songs gave us you, and then they took away your father and mother."* These words, found in pre–1949 editions of the work, were deleted from the final 1983 revision.

p. 109: *"tigers' ears": saxifrage.* Saxifrage "splits rocks"; it grows in cracks. Now prized as decorative potted plants, most Chinese species that are called "tigers' ear plants" (*huercao*) have fan-like leaves the shape of cats' ears, with soft down and a pink underside.

p. 139: *"had a chance for success in this."* The Chinese expression for *success* in this phrase, set off in the original in quotation marks, uses the word *border,* as in *Border Town.*

p. 156: In his penultimate revision of the novel for the Jiangxi People's Press in 1981, Shen replaced the final lines of chapter 20, beginning with "The old Daoist priest," with the expanded passage below. He deleted the addition from the final, 1983 version.

> The old Daoist priest, a literatus of *tongsheng* status who had changed his trade only after the 1911 revolution, mumbled to himself in bed, incoherently: "The emperor values literary renown; admonishes you people to get it for your own; other pursuits are all beneath us; only book learning commands us to bow down . . . Is it daylight? Time to rise and shine!"

Under the old monarchy, a *tongsheng* was merely qualified to sit for examinations that might lead to the *xiucai*, the minimal degree that conferred lower or sub-gentry status. What the old Daoist recites while waking was written in earnest by Wang Zhu (Northern Song dynasty) at the opening of his "Shen tong shi" ("Poem of the Boy Genius"), but, having been excerpted in elementary primers of the Ming and Qing dynasties, it had by the twentieth century become a stale homily memorized by Chinese children on the path to literacy. Admonishments to study Confucian classics sounded clichéd, pompous, and hypocritical to Shen Congwen's generation.

HARPER PERENNIAL
MODERN CHINESE CLASSICS

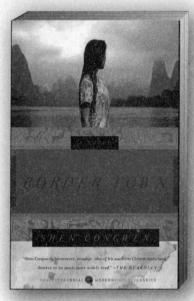

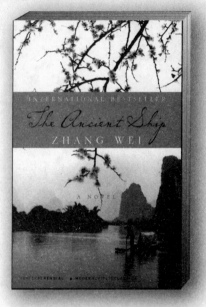

BORDER TOWN
A Novel
Shen Congwen

ISBN 978-0-06-143691-8 (paperback)

Cuicui, a young country girl coming of age during a time of national turmoil, dreams of finding true love, but is also haunted by the imminent death of her grandfather, a poor and honorable ferryman who is her only family. As she grows up, Cuicui discovers that life is full of the unexpected and she alone will make the choices that determine her destiny. First published in 1934, this beautifully written novel is considered Shen Congwen's masterpiece.

"Congwen's bittersweet, nostalgic tales of his southern Chinese homeland, pulled apart by civil war and revolution in the early 20th century, deserve to be much more widely read."   —*The Guardian*

THE ANCIENT SHIP
A Novel
Zhang Wei

ISBN 978-0-06-143690-1 (paperback)

Originally published in 1987, two years before the Tiananmen Square protests, Zhang Wei's award-winning novel is the story of three generations of the Sui, Zhao, and Li families living in the fictional northern town of Wali during China's troubled post-liberation years. Translated into English for the first time, *The Ancient Ship* is a revolutionary work of Chinese fiction that speaks to people across the globe.

"Beautiful and vivid . . . . The novel is witty and poignant, an epic spanning half a century of life in the fictional town of Wali."   —*The San Francisco Chronicle*

HARPER ● PERENNIAL
Available wherever books are sold, or call 1-800-331-3761 to order.